PENGUIN M.
LOVE WILL FIND A WAY

Anurag Garg is an engineering graduate and works in the IT industry. He's the author of two national bestselling novels, *A Half-Baked Love Story* and *Love . . . Not for Sale*. He loves to be close to nature and believes in creating circles of love and service around him. He lives in Delhi with his family.

You can follow him on Facebook/Instagram/Twitter:
www.facebook.com/anurag2392
www.facebook.com/AuthorAnurag
www.instagram.com/anurag_dreamer
www.twitter.com/anurag_stories

Or drop in a mail at:
anurag.stories@gmail.com
anurag2392@gmail.com

To know more about the author, visit:
anuragdreamer.wordpress.com

LOVE
WILL
FIND
A WAY

ANURAG GARG

Penguin
metro reads

An imprint of Penguin Random House

PENGUIN METRO READS

USA | Canada | UK | Ireland | Australia
New Zealand | India | South Africa | China

Penguin Metro Reads is part of the Penguin Random House group of companies
whose addresses can be found at global.penguinrandomhouse.com

Published by Penguin Random House India Pvt. Ltd
4th Floor, Capital Tower 1, MG Road,
Gurugram 122 002, Haryana, India

Penguin
Random House
India

First published in Penguin Metro Reads by Penguin Random House India 2017

ISBN 9780143439936

Typeset in Sabon by Manipal Digital Systems, Manipal
Printed at Repro India Limited

www.penguin.co.in

MIX
Paper from
responsible sources
FSC® C047271

'Once you choose love, anything is possible.'

Love you, Mom and Dad!

To Gitanjali,
I don't know if there's anything beyond right and wrong.
What I do know is that I want to be with you.
I love you, beyond forever!

Prologue

10 July 2016
New Delhi Railway Station

As soon as the delayed train reached the platform, passengers rushed to board. We quickened our pace as clouds began to gather in the sky. Looking up, I saw insidious grey encroaching on the blue expanse. The city was ready to welcome its first rain.

As the first few drops fell, we entered the carriage along with the other disgruntled passengers. When we found our berth, Gitanjali grabbed the window seat, as always, and asked me to buy a bottle of water from one of the stalls in the platform after placing our luggage in the overhead bin. I gave her an exasperated look. She looked outside as raindrops began to trickle down the window pane. She was wearing a pair of skinny black jeans and a turquoise T-shirt. Her warm chestnut hair rested on her neck and her long eyelashes swept alluringly against her rouged cheeks, from time to time.

'Get me a packet of chips, too.' She thoroughly enjoyed it when I catered to her every need, especially when we were on vacation. Three years into our relationship and we still bickered like teenagers! I handed her the requested goods while she plugged in her headphones.

I rummaged through my bag to find my neck pillow and settled down with my Saadat Hasan Manto book as the train pulled out of the station.

There was a couple with two children in the seats next to us. We exchanged smiles as a man selling tea came our way. They attempted to engage me in small talk even though I tried to keep to myself and buried my head in my book. Gitanjali, however, adores making conversation. With her legs folded under her and her hands gesturing wildly, her face glows when she narrates one of her tales. She began talking to the couple and playing with the kids. It made me immeasurably happy seeing her bright eyes and animated smile.

The TTE came to check our tickets.

'They're on your phone,' I said to her, as she continued playing with the little boy.

'No, they're not with me, Anurag,' she said, her attention focused on playfully tickling the boy, oblivious to the TTE who was breathing down our necks. She turned to me when the little boy suddenly started crying.

'Were you asking for the tickets?' she asked as she showed the TTE the IRCTC message on her phone. I heaved a sigh and said, 'Thank you, madam!' Gitanjali just smiled and began consoling the wailing kid. She had this uncanny ability to comfort those around her.

Just as the train left the Anand Vihar station, I went to the toilet to change into comfortable clothes for the long journey ahead since mine were slightly wet from the rain. On returning to our compartment, I saw a beautiful middle-aged woman sitting there, dressed in a floral knee-length kurta and smart trousers. I presumed she had boarded at Anand Vihar. The woman wore spectacles and had green eyes, just like Gitanjali. As she smiled at me, I was struck by an eerie feeling, as though I somehow knew her.

Most of the passengers were going to their home towns for the summer vacations, whereas some of them, like us, were going to Nainital on holiday. We had to get off the train at Haldwani, which was the closest town to Nainital, from where we had to take a taxi or bus to reach the hill station. I gazed at the scenic vistas as the train trundled through the countryside.

In Amroha, we saw farmers harvesting crops and cows grazing in the paddy fields. Little huts made of bamboo and mud dotted the scenes that rushed by. Gitanjali nudged me as I wrote down the plot points for my next book.

'Have you decided on the theme of the story?' she inquired loudly.

'Yes, I've been thinking about something . . . but I'm not sure. I want my character's motives and emotions to be driven by some sort of psychological disorder.' My words drew the attention of the beautiful woman and she looked up curiously from her book.

'I don't know, Gitanjali. I can't think any more. I am out of ideas,' I said, frustrated, looking out of the window, hoping the trip to Nainital might clear my mind. A couple of minutes passed as we continued discussing the plot. The woman opposite us occasionally glanced at us, but remained reticent.

'I just don't know how to take my idea further,' I said.

'Perhaps I could tell you a story?' The woman finally broke her silence. Her voice had an enchanting inflection.

I wondered if I should squander my time listening to her story but, perhaps, this was the right time, the right place and these were the right people to help me figure out my book. I believe that a story often chooses its writer.

'Yes, please,' Gitanjali gleefully agreed on my behalf.

'This is not a conventional story. It deals with more than just a disorder. It deals with discovering buried secrets, lost relationships and the power of love,' she said, putting her book aside.

'That sounds fantastic! I mean, why not? We want to hear your story for sure,' Gitanjali exclaimed. She lived for serendipitous moments such as these.

'It might take a good while, perhaps the next few hours, till we reach Haldwani,' the woman cautioned. Her low voice was like that of a midnight radio jockey. She was so captivating that we couldn't say no to her.

Gitanjali folded her legs under her and cupped her chin. I looked at the woman who had briefly closed her eyes. The train seemed hushed now. The sky morphed from grey to a burnt orange, piercing the rivers and streams that ribboned through the forests outside. The woman sighed and began to speak.

1

7 December 2011
New Delhi

Everything looked and sounded unreal. Nothing was as it should be. That's what I wanted, to be alone with myself in another world where the truth was untrue and life could hide from itself.

As Madhav read these lines, sipping the last of the whisky in his glass, he wryly thought about how these words had seemed more tangible earlier. He was a tall, fine-looking man with dark brown hair and eyes that had the startling clarity of a mountain stream. His features were sharply defined, especially his lips, which at the moment eagerly sought the alcohol.

It was the time of the night when the dark turns oppressive. A dimly lit lamp in his cosy room illuminated the tiny raindrops on his window. The cold moon was peeking through the clouds, barely discernible in the tar-black sky. Other than the petrichor emanating from the grass outside, he could only smell the whisky on his breath. He had been trying to write a collection of poems for four years now, a glaringly futile endeavour. He was stagnating in an abyss of alcohol and self-loathing.

Staring at the calm face of the Buddha on his wall, Madhav felt a violent urge rise up inside him.

'I cannot write.' He told himself this every other night. The last time he had written a somewhat meaningful poem was ten years ago. He attributed the present success of his poetry blog to the trending misanthropy among the angsty youth. Moreover, it probably became popular because the blog's name was, almost absurdly, *Love Makes Me Angry*. He never thought he would feel this kind of loneliness despite having hundreds of Facebook followers. But he did.

He had been a happy-go-lucky person once. Years ago, he'd enjoyed the company of his friends and family. But the suppressed itch of mistrust and insecurity had destroyed his will to socialize and connect with the world. He was still talkative and engaging but inherently wary of revealing his true views to anyone. There was something else, something strange he could feel in himself but could not express.

Many regarded his mood swings and bitterness merely as symptoms of his millennial angst. But that did not begin to compare with his daily self-inflicted torture of goading his reflection in the mirror, reiterating his own worthlessness. He would then refuse to reply to anyone's texts, avoid nights out and conversation, preferring to wallow instead, convinced everyone was better off in his absence.

Immersed in the memories of his past, he went through his e-mails and found one response to his poetry submission.

Dear Madhav Mehra,

We hope you're doing well. We read your synopsis and unfortunately it doesn't fit our publication criteria. We wish you the best for your future projects.

Another publisher had rejected him. Well, he was used to it by now. A feeling of loneliness plagued his every waking moment. It was this that blurred his thought, rendered his creativity impotent and saturated his soul. It was present when people lauded his achievements at parties. The only questions that echoed in the twenty-five-year-old's mind were, 'Who is Madhav? What does he actually want to achieve? What led to this state?'

He read another e-mail.

Hey, Madhav! I love your poems. I was crying by the end of it. I feel like I'm stuck in this vicious cycle too.

Such e-mails and messages made him shudder. There were thousands of them and they dogged his thoughts even though he tried to ignore these strangers' attempts to resonate with his art.

He poured some more whisky into his glass, and tried to empty his mind. He played some Bob Marley as the alcohol's familiar burn began to overtake his senses.

He closed his eyes, his lids weighing down heavily. Something was consuming his thoughts, something he had never shared with anyone.

He'd recently moved into a room on the terrace of his family's house. He had just finished the last semester of MBA from Delhi College of Management Studies after completing his graduation from an engineering college, where he was the university topper. Companies had started visiting the campus and he was supposed to suit up for an interview with a big marketing firm. He went through the guidelines he had received from the person in charge of training and placement.

He couldn't find a reason to stay awake. No words, no friends, nothing except those fan mails and a nagging girlfriend.

He went out on to the terrace and looked at the sky exhaling its last few spurts of rain before the onslaught of the Delhi winter. He gazed upwards, but could not see any stars.

He returned to his room, gulped down another glass of whisky and stood in front of the mirror placed in a corner of his room; the only thing that he would talk to at night. He stared at his face, framed by thick black-rimmed spectacles. His vision started to blur. He realized with a slight jolt that he'd become markedly lean and pale. The image became hazier. He placed his hand on the mirror and slowly caressed the bearded cheek in his reflection.

'How are you?' he asked the image.

Suddenly he saw someone else in the mirror. 'Please save me, Madhav,' said the image. Madhav jerked back, terrified, and fell to the floor. He stood up and looked at the mirror. The image was erect and staring at him. He tried to speak, despite his swollen tongue.

'Why are you here?'

'Because I will always be with you.'

'Please leave me alone, please . . . please,' he said to himself, hunched on the floor, until the whisky took its toll and he fell asleep. His mother, who later came to check on him, peeked through the keyhole and found him lying on the floor.

Madhav woke up the next morning to the sound of the housemaid shouting. 'A hundred times I've told him not to shove the garbage behind his bed. He's completely out of control,' she complained to Madhav's mother. Snigdha Mehra, Madhav's mother, was a housewife. She used to be a banker like her husband, but being in the same office had created friction between the couple and so she eventually quit. Madhav's parents had sent him and his elder sister, Vihana, to different boarding schools when they were quite young. Somehow, even on their return to Delhi, the family had never really reconciled as a whole. They lived under the same roof, struggling with each other, every single day.

His mother placed his breakfast on the table in his room and left. Last night had been his parents' anniversary. He hadn't attended the family dinner, choosing, instead, to lock himself in this room, as he had done so often these past few months.

Madhav realized he'd forgotten to put the whisky bottle back in his cupboard, but his mother had ignored its presence, just as she had ignored all his other misdoings. He once used to be famous for his good looks, dark poems and gold medals. But he had always felt incomplete. And now he repeatedly suffered from blackouts and fits of violent anger. His parents were worried for him as they knew there was something strange about him.

He took a quick shower and slipped into his formal clothes. He picked up all his certificates and put them in a sling bag. Walking towards the door, he felt as though his limbs were being controlled by an unseen puppeteer.

'I have an interview today,' Madhav announced to his father, mother and sister who sat at the dining table. His father, Yashveer Mehra, was one of those typical dads who'd spent a lifetime earning money and only realized later in life how much he valued his family. His beautiful sister, Vihana, was a PR manager in the US. She lived abroad with her boyfriend; she was in Delhi for a project.

'Which company?' his father asked, his eyes still fixed on the front page of the *Economic Times*.

'Ernst & Mark,' Madhav replied and sat down on the couch. His father adjusted his glasses and looked at him.

His sister, who was chatting with her boyfriend on the phone, said, 'I hope you're well prepared,' without even looking at him.

'Yes, better than you. You should focus on getting married,' snapped Madhav, as he turned on the television. She threw him a scathing glance.

'Will you have breakfast? I have left some on the table upstairs,' his mother said gently. Madhav nodded.

'Yeah, I know. I forgot to eat it. I'll have some here,' he said, rearranging his certificates.

His mother went to the kitchen and mixed some crushed antidepressants into his milk, the way she had been doing for a long time now. His family had been secretly treating Madhav with medication as per a psychiatrist's advice. According to the doctor, Madhav had suffered mental trauma in the past, which had manifested in a psychological disorder.

'Just be calm. You will breeze through it,' his mother said, mustering all the love she had for her son as she handed him the glass of milk. She touched his cheek as her eyes teared up. She had seen him prowling on the streets, abusing people, fighting with strangers and talking to his reflection in the mirror. She missed the boy her son used to be years ago.

Madhav left for college feeling confident. He knew his credentials could easily get him this job. He had not quite noticed his transition from wannabe poet to overachiever in college, but over the years, he had somehow lost the ability to express himself on paper.

In the metro, he sat and observed people, their conversations, their happiness and their worries. He wanted to express himself too but felt intensely stifled in the crowd. He sighed and looked out of the window.

Madhav finally reached his campus where plenty of final-year students were waiting, dressed for the interview. They all walked towards the auditorium for the company orientation.

The panel introduced itself to the eligible students and described the selection process. Madhav's meritorious grades were a great advantage for him and his professors already knew he would top the university in the final exams.

At the end of the orientation, the students were asked to report at the admin block for the interview.

'All the best, bro,' said Tanmay.

He was Madhav's only friend, although hardly so any more. They had met in first year and Tanmay had patiently endured Madhav's fluctuating temperament. He knew there was something disturbing Madhav deeply, and yet he had supported him in his silly fights, but Madhav, ungraciously, had always ignored his support. Tanmay wanted to help his friend get better, but Madhav never shared his thoughts or issues with him. Instead, he would shout or insult Tanmay whenever he asked about his past. As time progressed, Tanmay, too, started retreating from his life, just as everyone else around him had.

'I wish you all the best for whatever comes your way.' Tanmay was going to Germany for further studies. Madhav looked at him and said, 'Thanks. Take care. Fuck some Germans!'

'Maddy baby,' said a simpering voice from behind him. It belonged to a girl wearing denim shorts and a tight black top that complemented the curves of her body. Tanmay said hi to Meera and left.

Meera Raheja, Madhav's junior in college, was a gorgeous twenty-two-year-old with kohl-black hair that skimmed her shoulders. Her plump lips and slender eyebrows perfectly framed her face.

She had moved from Agra to Delhi after doing BCom to study management, but along the way, the speed and glamour of the city had shifted her focus towards other things.

Madhav first saw Meera at her fresher's party, where she was voted Miss Fresh Face. She had been surrounded by besotted classmates, but had eyes only for him. He was rich, attractive and intelligent and, thus, had all the prerequisites to hook up with Meera. Although she was fed up with Madhav's moodiness, she put up with it because she got everything she needed from him. He would pay her bills, her rent and fulfil all her weekly shopping requirements. Meera had often told Madhav that she had fallen in love with him, but he had never reciprocated her feelings.

Madhav tried to summon up some enthusiasm as he greeted her.

'You're looking dope AF, baby.' Millennial slang was her preferred language. 'I wish I could devour you.'

Madhav grabbed her waist and pulled her closer, drawing stares from the sexually frustrated crowd of single boys and girls.

'Look at her ass, bro,' said a boy in the crowd, staring at Meera's behind. Madhav overheard the lecherous comment and, handing his file to Meera, stormed off in his direction.

'What did you just say?' he asked the scrawny, pimply boy. Madhav was known for his short temper. He had had innumerable fights for no apparent reason in his two years at college and this was partly the reason why he had no friends.

'Nothing, bro. Just look at her ass. I feel like spanking her hard.' The guy clearly didn't know that Madhav was her boyfriend. His friends asked the guy to shut up but he continued laughing. That was the last straw. Madhav grasped his collar, punched the gangly boy's nose and kicked his ass. The guy and his friends fled to escape Madhav's wrath.

'Run home and you'd better watch your swollen ass,' Madhav said as the crowd laughed nervously. Meera ran towards Madhav and tried to calm him down.

'Easy, baby! Your interview is coming up. Let people stare.' She couldn't deny the pleasure she derived from any sort of male attention, a trait that Madhav had never been able to handle.

Meera was one of those girls who were admired from afar by everyone on campus. Guys would stare at her while girls were envious of her looks. Madhav's academic profile and dark poetry had caught her attention shortly after she began college. As for Madhav, she reminded him of someone from his past.

By the time Meera joined college, Madhav had become notorious for his capricious temper and frequent brawls. Madhav wasn't sure why she was with him. People said that she was simply using his popularity to remain relevant in the college gossip circuit. Madhav didn't pay any attention to this sort of talk. Although, he had to admit, the physical pleasure she gave him was pretty much the only reason he wanted to be with her.

'Are you free tonight?' he asked her. 'We can go to Zoo bar after I'm done with this fucking interview.'

'I am always free for you, my love,' she said, trailing a crimson-tipped finger down his cheek. The crowd thoroughly appreciated the PDA.

Madhav obsessively adjusted his tie until the HR head called out his name.

'Your turn, baby,' Meera said as she planted a kiss on his cheek. The security guards gave them dirty looks.

Madhav headed towards the room where the interviews were being held. There was a long line of students standing in the corridor, all mugging answers to questions they might be asked during the interview. The geeks stared at him as he walked towards the interview room. People found it hard to believe that someone like him was the university topper—a loafer who spent his time writing shitty poems for his blog. Madhav felt neither overconfident nor scared. He just wanted to look good for the interview.

The HR executive checked his college ID and faked an encouraging smile. He entered the room. Three people sat at a conference table—a middle-aged man, an old man and a beautiful lady.

'Good morning,' said the middle-aged man. He appeared to be the manager.

Madhav nodded and adjusted his spectacles. He wore spectacles that blurred his vision; he didn't really need them, but insisted on wearing them.

'You can at least wish us good morning, young man,' said the old guy. Madhav felt his sense of decorum beginning to waver.

'What's so good about this morning, sir?' he asked impertinently. The three company executives raised their eyebrows. Madhav had certainly captured their flagging attention with this response, but not in a favourable way.

'This is a rather negative approach, Mr Mehra,' the lady admonished.

'No, madam, this is actually the bitter truth. I wasn't able to go to the toilet in the morning and now I have stomach cramps, which you might unfortunately have to deal with in a bit. I did not eat breakfast. Another publisher rejected my poetry last night. And I lost my favourite pen. So, you see, for me it's not a good morning at all.' Madhav was only half-aware of what he was rambling on about, and the panel was extremely taken aback.

'Ridiculous! Are you out of your senses?' the lady berated him.

Madhav placed his file on the table. 'I am really very sorry, madam. Please take a look at my credentials.' It was impossible for anyone to predict his temperament. He would say something one minute and then do the exact opposite a minute later. People thought he was just a pathological liar, but nobody bothered to ask him why he behaved this way.

The two men flipped through his certificates and whispered amongst themselves. Madhav smiled all of a sudden.

'Tell us something about yourself.' The manager started the interview. Madhav was still standing, out of courtesy.

'I am Madhav Mehra.'

'We know your name! Tell us more about yourself.'

'I'm extremely confused.'

'Why are you here, then?'

'Because he wants me to be a slave to people like you,' said Madhav. This was blunt and unacceptable, especially as it came from the university topper. This was one of those situations wherein he knew he was going off track but couldn't help it. It was almost like an out-of-body experience. Madhav felt like a victim, trapped by his own emotions. He adjusted his spectacles and blurted out, unthinkingly.

'You know, this is the biggest problem with our nation—we all are in rooms like this one, trying to please someone who ranks higher than us. I'm in this room, trying to please you; the principal's secretary is trying to please him.' Madhav laughed as they looked at him in surprise.

He finally took a seat. 'Did I ask you to sit?' the old man questioned, even though he had pretty much given up on him by then.

'Do I seriously need your permission to sit? I mean seriously? This chair is meant to be sat on, right?' That was it. He had crossed the line.

'Do you even want this job?' the man asked, finally raising his voice.

'I don't. I never wanted it. He wants it. He's always wanted it,' Madhav declared and removed his spectacles.

'Who are you talking about? Who wanted it?' the woman asked.

'You will never know him,' he replied, as the old man called out for the college's HR and placement executives.

'I can't believe this is the topper of your college,' the lady said to the placement executive. They told the college officials all that Madhav had said and done. The

HR head then dragged him out of the room. After a long discussion, the placement cell blacklisted Madhav, despite him being the university topper. Madhav smirked and walked out of the campus gates.

2

Madhav did not tell his family about the interview but he couldn't hide the results of his final semester exams. He had topped yet again and, to lighten the tense atmosphere at home, his mother planned a small get-together.

Standing naked in front of the full-length mirror in his room, Madhav tried to figure out why he was so irked by all this appreciation. And then the usual questions began to harangue him yet again—who the hell am I? What have I really been doing with my life?

He stared deeply into his eyes, scrutinizing his irises, and rolled his eyeballs back into his head. And thus began his daily routine of self-deprecation.

A knock on the door jolted him back to the unwelcome present.

'Madhav, come out! Everyone is waiting for you,' a female voice shouted, knocking thrice on the door. Madhav wrapped a towel around his waist and ran to

open the door. It was his mother, in a beautiful cotton
sari. She looked happier than usual that night. Her son
had topped his college. It was a dream come true for her
but she, of course, wasn't aware that she had shared this
dream with someone else, someone whom she had never
really known.

'What are you doing, Madhav?' she asked, opening
the door wider. 'Why aren't you dressed yet?'

'For what?'

What a strange question!

'Son, there's a small party for you downstairs,' she
said gently, placing her hand on his cheek. Nobody could
say for certain what it was that he was going through,
because his symptoms were so odd. Every doctor would
attribute his condition to a different disorder. And his
stellar academic record only confused them further—
how could a university topper be mentally ill?

Madhav nodded and closed the door. He slowly
walked to and fro in front of his cupboard, eventually
picking out a round-necked T-shirt and shorts for the
party. It was difficult even for him to discern what he was
thinking when he took most of his decisions. He looked
like a child in that attire, maybe because he felt like one.
He applied some hair gel and wore his canvas shoes. He
kept his spectacles in his pocket. Sighing in anticipation
of the honeyed praise he would receive, Madhav dragged
himself downstairs. He received a few cheers and a few
whispers and sniggers at his outfit, but couldn't bring
himself to give a damn.

His mother walked towards him, past all the uncles and aunts with grave expressions on their faces, and asked, 'What have you done?' Madhav just shrugged, not entirely sure what she was referring to.

His mother tried to suppress her annoyance towards him and pretend as if everything was normal. She held his hand and led him to the party. His father hugged him tightly and clapped him on the back, presenting him proudly to the other guests. One of his uncles handed Madhav a bottle of champagne and said, 'Cheers!' The bottle sat heavily in his hand, like the weight at the bottom of his stomach.

'Madhav, why the hell are you wearing this shit?' whispered Meera in his ear. Her prickly voice pierced through him. She had come to the party at his insistence.

'I don't know.' Madhav finally broke his silence. He popped open the champagne bottle as the guests applauded. Meera stormed into the kitchen to check on the cake.

There were around thirty people present at the party, all close relatives and friends. Madhav's parents looked incredibly proud of their son's achievement. But Madhav's head was aching rather badly. The music was loud and the dim lights didn't help. Suddenly, Meera dragged him into an empty room. She closed the door and hugged him.

'What are you doing? Is everything okay?'

'Everything's perfect, my little schoolboy.' Meera tried teasing him but it turned out to be a bad move;

her words touched a nerve. Madhav leaned forward, roughly grabbed Meera's chin and bit her lips so hard that she screamed. With a knock on the door, Madhav's mother entered the room. 'What happened?' she asked, concerned.

Madhav immediately moved away from Meera and began fixing his hair. 'Nothing, Aunty, we were just playing around, pinching each other,' said Meera, to cover up what he had done.

'Let's go outside, everyone must be waiting for dinner,' said Madhav, feeling a little more in control. Meera wasn't sure if he was pretending to be ignorant; she had been privy to his unusual behaviour for a while now.

As they walked into the dining hall, an aunt whom he had hardly ever spoken to before, said, 'This is an amazing accomplishment, Madhav. This is what you've always wanted, right?'

'I never wanted this,' replied Madhav, curtly.

'What? What do you mean?' asked the maddeningly curious aunt.

'You heard me,' he said. He then laughed suddenly and placed his hand on his aunt's bare back. She squirmed and stepped back in discomfort.

The party ended soon after dinner. Madhav's parents bid the guests goodbye with boxes of chocolates. The numerous fake smiles and pretentious warm hugs left a grave silence in their wake.

'What were you doing, Madhav? Look at your outfit, look at your behaviour!' shouted Madhav's sister, the minute the last guest left.

'What's the matter with you guys? Did I ask you to celebrate? Did I ask you to call these fucking curious relatives?' he yelled back.

'Mind your language, Madhav!' said his dad.

'Why aren't you happy, *beta*? What has happened to you?' His mother caressed his head lovingly.

'I never wanted to become the person I am now.' Madhav's eyes narrowed dangerously as he spoke. 'It was always him, it is him even now. He wanted all of this and I am telling you to stay away!' He screamed as he ran up the stairs, leaving his family dumbfounded.

~

Madhav sat on an aluminium bench outside the doctor's office, relentlessly tapping his feet, trying to dry his sweaty palms. He was at Doctor Batra's clinic. Batra was a child psychiatrist, but Madhav's parents, oblivious to the difference between child and adult psychiatrists, insisted on taking their son to him. They were inside with the doctor, while Madhav awaited his turn. His sister, too, had come along, though she was in the corridor, talking to her boyfriend on the phone.

Anxiety overwhelmed Madhav during each of these visits. He constantly feared that one of these quacks would somehow manage to unearth his secret.

His thoughts wandered as he looked around at the other patients. When he was younger, he had believed the lie his parents had fed him about these visits being general consultation sessions for the whole family. But that façade had been dropped a while ago.

Madhav looked around the small clinic. The furniture was old and bruised. There were multiple posters on the walls asking patients to be aware of their mental health. 'Are you depressed?' probed one poster depicting a man with his head buried in his arms. There were several books and magazines in a corner next to a water tank that housed the most catatonic fish Madhav had ever seen.

The boy at the reception desk was slender and looked anaemic. Madhav stared at his back until he suddenly turned around. He quickly shifted his gaze, pretending to peruse a magazine titled *Peace of Mind*. As he flipped through the magazine, an article called 'Love Your Soul' caught his attention. Madhav felt a connection with every sentence in the article that delineated the importance of a symbiotic and nurturing relationship between one's soul and one's physical body.

He looked for the contact details of the author, but there seemed to be none. However, at the bottom, he found her name—Radhika Kapoor. But there was no picture.

'Radhika Kapoor,' Madhav murmured as the pale receptionist looked at him again. He tried to commit the name to memory.

Behind the closed chamber door, the doctor asked Mrs Mehra multiple questions about her son's recent behaviour. He read Madhav's case file that had the findings and opinions of several other doctors.

'Madhav repeatedly insists that he doesn't want this life. He says he is living for someone else. He talks to the mirror at night,' said his mother, her voice cracking. Madhav's father held her hand tightly.

'I need to talk to him. We should put him on stronger medication,' the doctor said as he wrote out a prescription.

'He is sitting outside, doctor.'

'Call him in,' the doctor said as he turned on his recording device.

His mother came out and saw him sitting impatiently, rubbing his palms together.

She went up to him. 'Madhav, the doctor is calling you.'

'I don't want to answer his stupid questions yet again,' Madhav replied, agitated.

'It will be fine, Madhav. He just wants to speak to you.' She lightly squeezed his shoulder.

'Oh yeah, I know. It will be all right the way you always claim it'll be, and then I won't remember anything the next morning.'

'Please, Madhav. Come for us. It will be fine,' she said, her eyes pleading.

Madhav faked a half-smile and went into the room with her. It was a spacious room with a desk and a small bookshelf. He had lain on the bed in the room before, next to which were several medical instruments.

Get-well cards were meticulously displayed along the windowsill, flanked by flower arrangements. How generic, he thought.

'Hello, Madhav! How are you?' the doctor asked, placing Madhav's case file aside as he rose to shake his hand. Dr Batra was a somewhat corpulent man in his mid-sixties who had been practising psychiatry for forty years and, yet, he hadn't been able to fathom Madhav's condition. According to him, Madhav was probably suffering from bipolar disorder and the only cure for that was strong medication and psychotherapy. He insisted on asking him the same questions during every visit, despite Madhav's evident frustration. But Mrs Mehra was hopeful that one day the psychiatrist would actually break through her son's peculiar shell.

'I'm fine, as always,' Madhav said, trying to be cordial.

Initially, Madhav answered all of Dr Batra's questions with great solemnity. Then he started joking about how college was making his life miserable. The more he talked, the more evident was his sadness. His voice became less domineering and more childlike. He told the doctor about a few of his insecurities—how a new job might restrict his creativity and affect his poetry and how certain expectations were starting to make him feel claustrophobic.

'How's your life, honestly?' Dr Batra asked another vague question to help Madhav open up a bit further.

'It's good.'

After a long pause, Madhav began to cautiously describe his rapid mood swings, delusions and insomnia. His appetite had steadily decreased and he was losing weight. He described his rollercoaster emotions, which had begun oscillating even more after he'd started college. He had taken to drinking and smoking, sometimes excessively. Without any warning, he would have periods of intense loneliness and depression, and then sporadic fits of exuberant happiness. He would burst out in rage at people unexpectedly. But he always evaded the topic of his childhood whenever Dr Batra tried to swing the conversation that way.

'How was the party last night?' the doctor asked. Madhav squirmed at his question. His parents looked at the doctor, unsure of what their son's reaction meant.

Madhav started gnashing his teeth, which added to his parents' wariness.

Then he replied, 'It was amazing. I enjoyed myself a lot.'

'I heard you had a tough time at your first placement interview,' the doctor finally started probing deeper.

'Hmm.' Madhav tried to look nonchalant. He interlaced his fingers and started tapping his feet on the floor again.

'It seems you don't want to talk about it. Do you feel as if someone is controlling your actions?'

Madhav bit his lip, trying to control his anger. He felt as if the question was an attack. 'What do you want to know? Be clear!'

'Did you see anything that scared you? Did you see anyone? Did you hear anyone?' The questions coiled in the pit of his stomach.

'Who are you talking about? Whom should I have seen?' He began to worry that the doctor had somehow found out about his past. 'I don't want to speak to you. I want to leave.' Madhav stood up, abruptly. His father asked him to sit down but he pushed his hand away and tried to walk out of the room.

'Calm down, Madhav. Please take this medicine,' said Dr Batra, as he held out a pill to suppress his anxiety. Madhav refused but his parents forced it into his mouth.

Slowly, his body loosened up as the medicine coursed through his veins and he slumped into a chair, half-asleep.

'I am really scared, doctor,' his mother pleaded.

'Mrs Mehra, his case is very different. I think he is suffering from a stress disorder.'

'What is that?' Madhav's mother was hearing this diagnosis for the first time. 'He was fine and completely normal when he returned to Delhi after that incident ten years ago. In fact, he excelled academically,' she said. But she somehow knew that he wasn't normal at all, even back then.

'This happens sometimes, Mrs Mehra. Patients generally bury themselves in a task or goal and become obsessed with it. Madhav probably suppressed his emotions after the incident, but now it's starting to return.'

Dr Batra recommended a trial run of antidepressants, which he said would hopefully help control Madhav's manic symptoms and normalize his sleeping patterns. He assured them that in a few days Madhav would be ready for outpatient therapy.

But fate had another path laid out for Madhav.

3

Tanmay found out about Madhav's deteriorating condition through Meera. She told him about the outburst at the party and what happened at Dr Batra's clinic.

Sometimes, people make a significant difference to our life in unexpected ways. Tanmay did his last bit before leaving for Germany by telling Meera about an art workshop. Called Art from the Heart, it was run by a foundation for which Tanmay had volunteered. 'Art therapy is a form of expressive therapy that uses the creative process of making art to explore our suppressed emotions,' explained Tanmay.

Meera thought this might help Madhav articulate his emotions better, so she planned to take him there. She decided she would tell him that it was just a run-of-the-mill art exhibition.

Madhav was on the couch, staring at his laptop blankly, as usual, when she called him.

'Hey, Meera!'

'Hey, how're you doing? Are you free to talk?' she asked.

'I'm in Sri Lanka now for a conference,' he replied.

'Stop it, Madhav!' Meera said, cautiously.

'Okay, tell me! My head is aching pretty badly.'

'I want you to come with me somewhere tomorrow. There's an exhibition by this artist called Radhika Kapoor. Say you'll come, please. It will be fun.' Her words tumbled over each other.

'An art exhibition? Are you serious?' he asked.

'Yes, I am damn serious,' replied Meera.

'That name sounds vaguely familiar though . . . Radhika Kapoor,' he said, scratching his head. Meera wondered if Madhav actually knew who she was and said, 'Oh! She's the founder of the Art from the Heart foundation.' Madhav immediately conjured up an image of Radhika Kapoor as a married, old woman who always smelt of heavily perfumed incense.

'I also wanted to ask you if I could use your latest blog post for my next project presentation.' Meera reverted to her selfish tone.

'Yeah, sure.' He couldn't care less.

'You are so sweet, Madhav! We'll talk later then. I am texting you the coordinator's number. Please register our names for the exhibition,' she said before she hung up.

Madhav was a little annoyed at the way she had spoken. He hesitated before calling the number she had sent him, but finally decided to go ahead. The caller tune was a religious song.

'Heelloo.' The man on the other end drew out the vowels of his greeting.

'Hi, is this Suresh?' Madhav asked.

'Yees,' Suresh drawled.

'My friend, Meera, and I would like to attend the art exhibition tomorrow. How do we register?' Madhav asked.

'Exhibition?' Suresh seemed perplexed. 'This is an art therapy workshop.'

'Art therapy?' Madhav was confounded by this information.

'Yes. We will be exhibiting your paintings, though. Are you the patient or is it Ms Meera?'

'What are you talking about?' Madhav sounded annoyed.

'How about I register you both?' asked Suresh. 'Greetings from Art from the Heart.'

Within five minutes, Madhav received details of the venue and a request to reach the premises by noon, a time when he was usually hung-over. So he decided not to drink that night, or to maybe drink a little less than usual.

He woke up early the next morning. He felt strange without the now all-too-familiar hangover. He felt vulnerable to the world around him, to himself. It had been a few days since his temper was last whipped into a frenzy, but it seemed as though something in him was going to explode soon. His phone rang.

'Morning, Maddy! Are you ready? Shall I come pick you up?' Meera asked, her voice animated as ever. He was somewhat pissed because she had lied to him about the art therapy session. But he decided to go along.

Madhav knew that Meera did not truly love him and often faked her affection for him but, at the same time, Meera's acceptance of his unusual behaviour made it easy to be with her. All that sex didn't hurt either.

'I will be ready in an hour. Call me when you're about to reach,' he said, disinterestedly.

'Okay, baby, I will give you a call,' she said. 'Looo . . .' He disconnected before she could complete her whiny 'Love you'.

Madhav suddenly felt in control that day. The air was crisp and the sun was shining brightly. But there was a curious tinge to the day. The smell of something like renewal, perhaps.

He got ready and went downstairs to see his family. The maid would now clean his room only after he left.

'Madhav!' His mother's eyes brightened on seeing him. 'Will you have breakfast?'

'Mom, can you please ask me some other question every morning?'

'Sorry, beta. But let me know. I'm making some for your father,' she said and went back to the kitchen. 'Where's Vihana?' he inquired.

'She's left for a meeting with a client.'

'I will have some toast,' he said finally, walking towards the kitchen.

'Where are you going today?' his mother asked.

'To an art exhibition.'

'With Meera?'

'Yes,' he said, as he munched on a chocolate cookie. He used to demolish entire jars of these when he was a kid.

'Do you like her?' she pressed further. That threw Madhav off.

'She's just a good friend.'

His mother nodded and buttered his toast for him. Madhav wrapped the slices in a tissue and left.

'Where are you, Meera? I have been waiting for you.' He was starting to get impatient.

'I can see you, love,' she said.

Meera brought the car to a squealing stop. The sound made Madhav turn around. Meera had come in her flatmate's car. She winked at him as he got in. She leaned in to kiss him but he turned his face away.

'What's going on, Maddy?' she asked, taking off her shades.

Madhav was still preoccupied with his mother's question. And now he couldn't stop asking himself if he loved Meera.

But all he said was, 'Nothing. Let's go.'

The question played in a loop in his mind. Meera kept nagging him but Madhav paid little attention and was relieved when they finally reached the venue. It looked like a school of sorts. A geeky-looking, over-enthusiastic girl stood at the gate with a placard that read 'Free Hugs'. Meera chuckled while parking the car. There were throngs of people entering the premises. It was like a huge, colourful fair.

'The exhibition looks great,' Meera said. Madhav glanced sideways at her, amused that she was still lying.

They entered the premises and found themselves in an inner courtyard bordered by large buildings and slender stairways. Unsure of where to go, she suggested he call up Suresh. Madhav heard the same religious ringtone but not the drawn-out hello. Instead, there was a woman's pleasant husky voice on the other end. She said hello, in a brisk yet seductive way.

'Umm, hello,' he stuttered.

'Hi, Suresh is in the prayer room. May I know who's speaking?'

'My name is Madhav. I'm here for the Art from the Heart exhibition and wanted to know where exactly to go.'

'Oh! Where are you? I will send someone over to bring you here.' Everything the woman said was infused with sincerity and warmth.

'We are at the main gate.'

'I'll see you soon.' Madhav felt a twinge deep in his stomach as she disconnected the call.

They waited for fifteen minutes before a young boy appeared before them. Clad in shorts and a ragged T-shirt, he stood there scratching his head and staring at Meera.

The boy's eyes shone with innocence and he smiled hesitatingly.

Madhav raised his eyebrows and asked, 'Are you from Art from the Heart?'

He turned to Meera, slightly bewildered, when the boy didn't reply. Perhaps he was shy.

'Are you here to take us somewhere?' Madhav asked again. The boy nodded this time.

The boy reached for Madhav's hand and held on to his fingers tightly. It felt odd, but comforting, this tiny hand in his. The boy started walking briskly, practically dragging Madhav along.

'Hey, slow down! What's your name, buddy?' Madhav asked him.

'Aakash,' he said, grinning broadly.

Walking through the campus, Meera and Madhav saw several different workshops taking place, creating a din that was both chaotic and calming. Madhav was surprised by his reaction to the boy taking his hand, at how this simple touch seemed to strike some latent chord within him. What he didn't know was that this gesture was the first part of the therapy.

They arrived at a tall building with colourful walls and origami cranes suspended from the ceiling. As Aakash led them up the stairs, they saw a huge sign that read, 'The Healthiest Form of Projection is Art'. Five words— faith, trust, love, dream and kindness—marked the last five steps that led to a semi-open terrace. It was a bright space with a huge terrace garden. The place was quiet and Madhav noticed people sitting in a circle holding hands, their eyes closed. In the centre of the prayer circle was a bust of the Buddha flanked by candles.

Aakash looked at Madhav and placed a finger on his lips. They removed their shoes and Aakash placed them along with the others that had been arranged in the shape of a heart.

The space exuded a strange and powerful energy. It almost scared Madhav. He looked for a place to sit while Meera settled into a corner. There was absolute silence in the room even though there were around twenty people in there. Madhav's gaze fell on a girl and remained fixed on her. She sat cross-legged, her back ramrod straight while she breathed deeply, her eyes closed. Her brown hair flew gently in the breeze.

Madhav managed to find a space to her left, and sat down, transfixed. He looked around and saw murals depicting the dreams of children and adults alike, dotted with whimsical doodles. Paper lamps and flowers littered the space, making it look cosy and warm.

Madhav tried to observe the other people in the circle, but his eyes were inexplicably drawn back towards the girl. She seemed to glimmer in the light of the candles and lamps. Her magnetic presence was easily felt, even with his eyes closed. He felt as though she was the only real person there.

A chant arose from the circle, breaking his reverie. The room echoed with a Buddhist mantra that rushed through his veins and prickled his skin. He opened his eyes before anyone else did and a murmur ran through the room. The girl uttered a soft chant and opened her eyes, which were large and spectacularly green—the green of trees and seas in dreams.

She was slender, with shoulder-length brown hair and pale skin. Although she wasn't tall, her angular shoulders and firm posture gave her a quietly determined look. She wore silk pants, loosely bound at the ankles, a loose white cotton shirt and a long silk shawl. All her clothes were of different hues and she wore her shawl backwards, with the smooth fabric flowing down her back.

'Thank you, everyone,' she finally spoke. It was the same voice he'd heard on the phone, husky and seductive. She folded her hands and greeted everybody in the circle with a bow. Her voice was almost a whisper. She looked around, at each one of them, and finally came to Madhav. As their gazes locked, they both drew a breath, the moment suspended between them. Then they exhaled and she looked away.

Madhav sat stunned. The light in her eyes evoked something deep within him—he felt as though her soul glinted in those orbs. As she smiled, she illuminated the whole circle with an ethereal glow. He began to wonder whether, despite his cynicism, love at first sight might actually exist. Perhaps this is what it felt like—a sudden bolt of energy, of magic.

'I offer my deep gratitude to this circle. We are blessed by your presence here. We have some new beautiful souls who have joined us today.' The girl's voice ebbed and flowed rhythmically.

'I'm Radhika Kapoor. I work for Art from the Heart and I welcome you all.'

She said her name with an impish glint in her eyes. Her crescent-shaped eyebrows rose slightly when she caught Madhav staring at her.

The curve of her smile spoke of a certain pride and confidence. Madhav felt that perhaps a lot of people mistook her pride for arrogance and confused her quiet confidence with impassivity. His thoughts were lost, swimming in the lagoon of her steady, even stare.

Suddenly, he felt someone's arms encircle him, pulling him into a long hug as he sat there dumbfounded, unsure of what was happening.

'Namaste, I'm Suresh. Welcome to Art from the Heart.' A tall man smiled at him as though he'd known Madhav for ages. Suresh looked like he was around twenty-five years old. But his deep wrinkles and conspicuously flabby stomach gave him the careworn look of a much older man. In defiance of the humid climate, Suresh wore baggy canvas trousers, a khadi kurta and a rumpled Nehru jacket. His thick, curly black hair skimmed his collar and the stubble on his tired face looked about three days old.

'So here at Art from the Heart, we paint our emotions. We paint what we feel. We hold art therapy sessions every month. The paintings around us were created by our previous participants. Perhaps you can see the emotions that influenced these canvases and that is what we want you to try to do today.'

Everybody was impatiently glancing around as Suresh's speech came to an end. There were some tangible moments of connection between the art on display and the people present. But Madhav's eyes were glued to Radhika.

'This white canvas is just like your life; it's entirely up to you how you wish to paint it. Each stroke of colour, each line you draw, represents the choices in your life. Painting exposes a bit of your soul to the people who see your work. Where words fail, colours and strokes convey. It is a way of connecting with your innermost self. And, more often than not, we surprise ourselves when we create this way,' said Radhika, holding up a plain canvas. Her hair rippled around her. She was lithe and fit.

The volunteers began handing out paints and brushes and setting up the easels. Madhav stood up and went up to Meera.

'Wasn't this supposed to be an exhibition?' He finally broke his silence, his tone cutting, even though he was rather glad to be there, having seen Radhika.

'Umm . . . yes, it is. I mean it's more like . . . Well, you always say you're an artist, right? So I thought . . .'

'I think both of you should start.' A sweet voice from behind interrupted. It was Radhika.

She turned to the group and clapped loudly, making an announcement. 'Okay, guys! We have forty-five minutes to complete this task. Just embrace the colours, the fluidity of the paint, the experience of creating something on a flat surface and bringing it to life. Listen to the story it is telling you . . . let the paint, the brush, the canvas, all come together to create this story, this memory.' She spoke with a childlike excitement, laughing and clapping with abandon. Madhav felt as if his limbs were numb, as though he was falling in a dream, but without the inevitable jerk of awakening that followed.

He went back to his assigned easel as the volunteers handed out slips of paper with instructions to the participants.

This activity will ask you to perhaps face some unpleasant moments in your life, but with the goal of realizing and accepting them.

Paint a loss in your life. If you've lost someone or something you love, try to narrate the experience through your canvas. This will help you to not only remember but also to begin healing.

Madhav felt his mouth go dry. His head started reeling with memories of that godforsaken day and he stood sweating, petrified of the consequences if he were to begin painting.

'What happened?' Radhika asked, placing her hand on his shoulder. Her touch sent shivers down his body, till his extremities were tingling.

'Nothing . . . I was just thinking.'

'Let it flow, Madhav,' she whispered in his ear. Madhav was surprised that she knew his name. He berated himself for going soft, just because he'd been touched by small gestures all day—from the little kid taking his hand to the random hugs in the circle.

Everybody began sketching on their blank canvases. Madhav looked at Meera. She was busy clicking selfies next to the canvas by brandishing the brushes and pouting. Though the instructions haunted Madhav, he decided to give it a try. He closed his eyes and sighed.

The sight that came to mind was painful. His fingers trembled as he picked up the pencil. He started drawing the memory he had most carefully guarded all his life, one which had become a crucial part of him over these years.

He let his mind dig into the sands of his past, slowly excavating the buried images. Every time he put the pencil to canvas, a new facet of the memory revealed itself to him. He didn't pick any of the colours before him; he was drowning in a monochromatic sea. He felt as if his soul was crawling out of his body and he was observing it from afar.

Covered with sweat, Madhav felt like the protagonist of an extravagant, complex play without a script. But he could feel his lips twisting, first into a smile and then a frown, oscillating with each stroke. He was a fugitive. He was free.

'Okay, everybody! Time is up,' Suresh declared. Madhav snapped out of his trance and, half-realizing what he'd done, stumbled to the edge of the terrace without looking at his painting. He held on to the railing tightly, his heart pounding. It was like he had lived a whole lifetime and then died in the last forty minutes, and he wasn't ready to be resurrected quite yet. He could hear kids shouting somewhere. He looked down and saw Radhika playing with children. She was dancing to her own made-up tune and clapping. He fell in love with that sight, and his heart beat returned back to normal, the sound of her laughter calming him.

'Madhav!' Suresh called him back to the group.

'Oh! Umm . . .' Madhav couldn't speak. His eyes were fixed on Radhika's face.

'Hope you had a great session. Thanks for coming! Do you want to interact with the kids?' Suresh asked.

'What? No, no. Sorry!' he said.

'You can go down and speak to Radhika.'

He couldn't have been happier.

He went downstairs, while Meera was asked to wait in another room.

Madhav walked across the playground towards Radhika. He walked with a purpose, not looking down even once, as if there was a magnetic force pulling him towards her. Suddenly he slipped. It took him a few seconds to figure out what was happening to him.

A pair of hands grasped his arm at the elbow and jerked him upright. He swung around to face his saviour. It was Radhika, the most beautiful woman he'd ever seen. Her hand was still resting in the curve of his arm, near his elbow.

He felt an almost irresistible urge to take her hand and place it flat against his chest, near his heart, and let her feel his heartbeat. Instead, they stood looking at one another for five infinite seconds, while all the possibilities of parallel worlds and lives whirled gently around them. Meera caught sight of them from the terrace.

Radhika slowly moved her hand away. It was an easy, relaxed gesture, but he felt the loss of her touch as startlingly as the awakening jerk after a fall in a dream. He then leaned towards her, trying to get a look at her back as the kids laughed at him.

'What is it?' she asked, amused.

'I'm looking for your wings. You are my guardian angel, aren't you?'

'I'm afraid not. I have heard these lines before,' she replied with a wry smile. 'There's too much of the devil in me for that.'

'Just how much of the devil?' Madhav asked.

One of the kids, the scrawniest one, stepped in between them and tugged at Radhika's shawl. 'Madam ji! Come on, let's play!'

She let slip a fake sigh and smiled at Madhav, shaking his hand firmly. He couldn't for the life of him figure out what she was thinking.

'Thank you!' he said, as her hand slipped away from his.

'Don't worry. I'm sure you'll find some way to repay the favour,' she replied. The kids had moved to the other side of the ground, and she went to join them. The children were all very young, urchin-like in their slightly tattered clothes. They laughed and leaned against one another familiarly, but no one touched Radhika. She seemed to project an aura that was simultaneously attractive and inviolable.

Madhav moved closer, pretending to enjoy watching the kids play. He listened as she spoke to them, but couldn't make out her words. Her voice was surprisingly deep and sonorous; the hair on his arms tingled at its timbre. Madhav was befuddled by his reaction to this woman.

She asked them to continue playing and then led Madhav back to the building.

'I hate leaving these kids, they love me so much,' she said as she tied up her sleek hair. Her white shirt now had a few streaks of dirt.

'I could see that. I've heard of you before, you know. I have read an article written by you. It was amazing,' Madhav said. Her green eyes pierced his heart as she looked at him.

'Thank you,' she said.

'Well, to be honest, I thought you were an old married woman. But you're beautiful . . . and so young and . . .' He was unable to form coherent sentences as she looked straight into his eyes.

'Thank you,' she said again.

'You don't seem very modest,' he said.

'I don't think modesty is a very good policy, unlike honesty.' There was confidence in her voice. 'I love appreciation. It helps me connect to the source of a person, sometimes even their heart. Like they say, beauty lies in the eyes of the beholder, so I love to connect with the beholder's eyes, not the beauty—the source rather than the observation.' Her words were too philosophical for him to comprehend. 'How was your painting session?' she asked.

'It was good. But I don't remember much of it,' he said. Radhika shot him a questioning look.

'Did you see my painting?'

'No, I didn't. It's not about the painting. It's about how you felt,' she half-lied to him. She was actually quite curious to see his painting.

'It was good. I mean, I don't know. Sorry, I'm feeling a bit light-headed,' he said. Radhika nodded and asked him to call it a day.

'So that's it?' he asked, wanting to keep the conversation going.

'Yes, that's enough for today. I'll see you soon.'

'Soon? When?' he pressed, eager to meet her again.

She bit her lower lip to suppress a smile. 'Soon, Madhav. Don't worry,' she said as they rejoined the group.

Meera had noticed the way Madhav had looked at Radhika. They didn't talk during the journey back to his place. He was quiet, thinking about his encounter with Radhika, while Meera seethed with resentment.

Meanwhile, Radhika and the other programme coordinators examined the paintings. They sat in a circle and discussed their observations. Radhika asked for Madhav's painting. Suresh picked up an unsigned canvas and handed it to her. All the participants had signed their works, except Madhav. She took the painting and contemplated choosing Madhav as her case study. She felt an inexplicable pull towards his energy and his mind.

She looked at the painting; it was a picture of two boys on a hilltop, looking away from the viewer, dressed in what seemed to be school uniforms. One of the boys was in a wheelchair. They seemed to be looking at a small building. A layer of dark clouds framed the upper half of the canvas. Radhika was baffled by the intensity and darkness of the painting, wondering what repressed feelings might have compelled Madhav to create something like this. The painting was difficult to decipher, but it clearly indicated an underlying story.

Who were these boys? Why had Madhav painted this? What was he hiding? The questions haunted Radhika as she gazed wordlessly at the painting.

4

Golden rays streamed in through the window as morning dawned. The curtains swayed in the breeze as Madhav lay in bed half-asleep.

'Please save me, Madhav.' The words resounded in his ears as he struggled to wake up. Even after he opened his eyes, he was certain someone was whispering behind him, repeating the phrase like a chant.

Madhav tried to regain control over his breathing. His laptop lay open on the floor. He could not remember falling asleep. Empty glasses and the remnants of a joint were scattered on the table.

He cringed as his phone rang shrilly. 'Meera calling!' the screen announced.

'Maddy baby,' she said, in what she apparently thought was a cute voice.

'Morning,' he said, struggling to keep his eyes open.

'Baby, why are you talking to me like this early in the morning?' she whined in the same tone.

'How should I talk then?' he asked, scratching his balls.

'At least say something sweet, na,' she implored. 'You haven't talked to me properly since we went for that stupid workshop.'

'Meera, grow up! And that workshop was not stupid.' He looked around for his spectacles.

He saw drops of blood on the white marble floor. Madhav told Meera he'd call her back.

'No, don't go. Please talk to me. You never give me the time of day any more,' Meera whined. She had been with Madhav for five months now. She had seen him in all kinds of moods and yet couldn't figure him out. She knew she wasn't allowed any glimpse into his true feelings.

Madhav disconnected the call while she was still talking. He bent over and touched the blood. The drops seemed to trail across the room, all the way to the terrace door. He slowly walked towards the door and his phone rang. It was Meera again. He ignored the call. An uneasiness crept up through him. He slowly opened the door to see a fog obscuring his view of the terrace. The air was cold and heavy.

He saw a dead rat lying on the doormat. It had been stabbed with a wooden pencil. It was his. Bile rose in his throat, but he somehow managed to resist throwing up. Using the pencil, he picked up the rat and threw it over the terrace railing. Returning to his bed, he tried to get rid of the grotesque image from his mind in vain—who the hell had stabbed the rat? He shivered at the possibility.

In an effort to distract himself, he logged on to Facebook to check out Radhika's profile. He saw a few candid photographs that she'd uploaded. He missed her presence. He then checked her relationship status which stated she was single. Madhav smiled.

On reading further, he found that she had studied psychology at Delhi University and then done her masters and doctorate in clinical social work from London. She had other degrees to her credit as well. What he wanted to know was her age; her birthday wasn't mentioned on her profile.

As he scrolled down her friends' list, he exclaimed, 'Over three thousand friends!' He sent her a friend request and immediately changed his profile photo to one in which he looked more contemplative. He updated his profile and sighed.

Much too impatient to even wait for her to accept, he sent her a message. '*I am not feeling well, doctor. I need your advice.*' He attached a winky face emoji.

To his surprise, he saw that she was typing a reply. His heart rate increased exponentially and he forgot everything else.

His phone rang. Meera again! He switched off the phone. As the torturous little dots danced on the screen, he flopped on to his bed.

'*Mr Mehra, the doctor is busy shifting into her new office today. So please make an appointment for next week.*' She too added a winky emoji. He smiled and tried to think of a witty reply.

'*But I'm missing the doctor*,' he began to type but stopped himself. It sounded too desperate; it was too early.

'*This patient could help his doctor with the shifting process if she'd like.*' He couldn't think of a better reply.

'*Your phone is switched off,*' she replied. He jumped to grab his phone and switched it on.

'*While my poor phone comes to life, you could accept my request,*' he wrote. She sent a grinning smiley.

'*But we are not friends yet,*' she replied. He sent a bawling smiley. She replied with a tongue-sticking-out face.

His phone rang. It was an unknown number.

'Hello, Radhika?' he asked, hardly able to breathe.

'Madhav Mehra?' a male voice asked, dampening his excitement.

'Yes.'

'I am calling from the college's training and placement department. You have been shortlisted by Emarket. They have called you for an interview even though you were blacklisted. The college administration has decided to give you one last chance since you are a gold medallist. We hope you will behave properly this time and will not let us down.' The man said all of this in one go, like in a terms and conditions advertisement.

'Oh. Yes, sir. I will.'

'We will mail you the details.' He disconnected the call. Madhav sat back thinking of the whirlwind that had been these last few days—the interview, Dr Batra's clinic, the party and yesterday . . . He was on the verge of slipping back into the familiar pit, but the prospect of hearing Radhika's voice kept him on the precipice.

As he waited for her call, Meera called him again.

'What are you doing, baby?' she asked, her voice sickly sweet.

'Nothing, I'm just sleepy,' he said, trying to avoid conversation. He cared less for her now than before.

'Come over, na. Maybe we could take a nap together,' she said, suggestively. To Madhav's surprise, he found himself refusing. This was unprecedented. Their entire relationship was based on sex and he had never before turned down such requests.

'No, Meera. Actually I'm busy today. I have an interview to attend and have to prepare for that,' he lied. He didn't want to tell her that he was probably going over to Radhika's office.

'Wow! That's great!' she trilled. 'Come over. I'll help you prepare.'

'No, I really don't feel like meeting anyone today. I'll see you later,' he said and disconnected the call. Lying on his back, he stared at the fan and began daydreaming about meeting Radhika again.

His phone beeped. It was a message from an unknown number.

'*New office: B/72, 2nd Floor, Civil Lines, Near Chancellor Building, DU Campus. Love, Radhika.*'

He smiled as he ran a hand through his hair.

His mother entered the room and seeing him smile, was overcome with happiness. She thought of asking if he wanted breakfast but didn't want to disrupt his pleasant thoughts. She just looked at him from afar, at the smile that she thought he'd lost for good.

~

Dressed in a black leather jacket, black jeans, a black polo shirt and white canvas kicks, Madhav drove to the Delhi University campus and parked his car in front of Radhika's office building. Weaving his way through a throng of students, he climbed the stairs to the second floor and went in, passing a sign that read, 'Keep both your shoes and ego off'. A Swiss cowbell tinkled charmingly above the door.

The place was awash with pleasing fragrances. His heart pounding, Madhav peeked into a huge room with white walls. A girl in a sleeveless floral kurta, navy blue cotton trousers and a bandana tied around her head was painting a cage with birds frozen in flight on a wall.

'Ahem,' Madhav tried to capture her attention. The girl turned around. It was Radhika. She looked beautiful, but he was distracted by a drop of white paint on her nose. He alerted her to its presence. Attempting to wipe it away, she unknowingly smeared more paint on her cheeks. She raised her eyebrows as Madhav laughed.

'What? Come inside, you fool,' she said, tossing her paintbrush on to a newspaper on the floor. The place was a mess, yet it looked beautiful.

Madhav stepped closer to her. They were inches apart when he pointed at her nose and said, 'You are painting your face along with these walls, and I don't know which looks more beautiful.'

He looked at her closely. Her eyelashes looked like velvet. She had nymph-like features: a slightly pointed ears, a dainty nose and pearly teeth. A cute dimple adorned her right cheek and a beautiful pin glinted on her nose. A pair of dangling earrings and a bandana completed her look.

She smiled a little and Madhav was swept away. The shape of her face was so perfect that every curve mesmerized him.

'You writers really don't miss a single chance to flirt, do you?' she teased.

'How do you know I write?' he asked, amazed.

'I know everything, Mr Mehra. I know that love makes you angry.'

He gave her a sheepish smile, suddenly ill at ease thinking about his angsty blog.

'There's still some paint left,' he said, attempting to shift her focus.

'Yes, I know.'

'I am talking about your nose.'

She chuckled again. 'You are funny, Mr Mehra.'

He brought his finger closer to her nose and, gathering all his courage, dabbed at it. It was so soft. He felt like planting a kiss where his finger had been. Controlling his emotions, he hid the writhing inside him with a smile.

'Is there no one else here?' he asked.

'Well, not right now. Maybe in a while,' she said as she went back to her painting.

'Do you know how to paint?' she asked.

'I guess you have not seen my painting yet.'

'No, I haven't,' Radhika lied to him. She had already begun to plan his therapy. She wanted to help him deal with his ghosts and resolve his issues.

'Do you want to see me paint today?' he asked.

She turned to him with the widest and most radiant smile he'd ever seen. 'Why not? Pick your colours and go ahead. Don't you dare spoil my walls, though!'

They both laughed. Madhav rolled up his sleeves and tried to sketch a tree near her cage. They shared a brief glance as they tried to look at one another surreptitiously but failed.

There was something in the warmth of her smile that pierced him, a kind of mischievous exuberance, more honest and exciting to merely be joy. It was during that shared glance that Madhav decided to trust this woman. While he didn't know it then, it was one of the best decisions of his life.

Radhika went over to the packed boxes and, after some contemplation, picked up a large one. It looked heavy but Madhav refrained from helping her since he thought she might construe it as flirting again. He finally gave in when he saw her face was visibly strained.

'May I help you?' he asked her.

'No, it's fine. I can manage,' she grunted, her womanly pride kicking in.

She looked into his eyes and asked, 'How much time do you have?'

He couldn't figure out what she meant.

'For how long do you think you're going to live?' She asked again.

'What? How do I know?' Madhav was shocked.

'Another thirty years or maybe thirty days?' she asked. Her brusque manner gave him goosebumps.

'Why are you asking me this?' he asked, perplexed. She did not answer and began unpacking the box. There were about fifty books in there, mostly on psychology.

'I love them,' she whispered and hugged one of the books.

He thought of asking, 'And me?' but resisted.

'Come on, let's have coffee,' she said and walked towards her open kitchen.

'So you don't have a girlfriend?' she asked, placing a cup of coffee in front of Madhav. 'I'm sorry. Was the girl at the workshop your girlfriend?'

'No, no, I'm single. I mean, she's a good friend. Not a girlfriend,' he mumbled.

'How is that possible?' Radhika needled him. 'Are you on Tinder?'

'What? No.'

'Show me your phone.' She was being surprisingly straightforward given that it was only their second meeting.

'Okay, I am,' he confessed.

'Looking for hook-ups, right?' She laughed.

'Oh come on! It's like Facebook.'

'Yes, it's the Facebook for horny people.' She continued laughing. 'Sorry, I'm just teasing you. Please have your coffee.'

As they shared a couple of jokes and stories, Madhav realized he hadn't felt this relaxed in far too long. The conversations, the smiles, even the playful bickering made him feel alive.

He took off his jacket, revealing his muscles. Radhika cocked her head slightly to one side. 'You like girls, don't you?'

'Well, yeah, sure,' he said, looking around in embarrassment. He caught sight of a tattoo on her exposed left shoulder. It looked like the tail of some animal.

'Well, yeah, sure,' she mimicked him and laughed. 'Good. It would've been a tragedy to womankind otherwise.'

Madhav didn't understand what she meant at first, and his ears burned when he finally caught wind of her suggestion. Her humour was extraordinarily open and unexpected. He couldn't look anywhere else but in awe at her.

'What if I say you're left with thirty days? How are you going to prioritize everything in your life?'

Madhav was thoroughly disconcerted by the abrupt shift in conversation. She was even more unpredictable than he'd thought.

He looked at her suspiciously as she raised her eyebrows. 'What do you mean? Why are we talking about this all of a sudden?'

'What I mean is very simple, Madhav. No matter how long you live, what matters is what you do in those years.' She laid her hand on his, her eyes pulsing with a strange energy.

'I'm not saying we have to live every day as if it's the last day of our lives. But we shouldn't become complacent thinking that we have all the time in the world to accomplish our dreams, because we really don't,' she said, sipping her coffee.

'Who has time for these questions? It's difficult enough keeping my head above water, trying to survive,' he said, gripping the table in frustration. How had this conversation gone from Tinder to life coaching?

'Do you want to live your life or just survive?' She held his hand tightly and caressed it. He sighed, trying to grapple with her complex questions.

'You know, something strange happened this morning,' he said, his thoughts wandering.

'What happened?' she asked, curiously.

'I woke up and saw drops of blood on the floor. As I followed the trail of blood, I found a rat that had been stabbed with a pencil. It was the same pencil with which I wrote every night,' he whispered.

Radhika listened to him carefully and thought about what he'd said for a minute. 'He must have committed suicide.' She tried to make light of it, making a mental note of the incident for future therapy, but Madhav remained shaken.

'Let's not talk about it any more,' she said. 'Finish your coffee.'

He hastily gulped down his coffee. She was like a mother, caring yet firm. Madhav wanted to know more about her life, her family, friends, everything.

'When are we meeting next? I mean, when is our next session?' he asked.

She gave him a half smile. 'When this office is done.'

'Not fair!'

'Let's go,' she said and got up.

As she switched off the lights, Madhav asked, 'Where are you headed now?' He tried to feign nonchalance.

'I live nearby, in the next lane. But I intend to shift into my office soon.' She took out a helmet from her bag as they moved downstairs. She had a scooter, a yellow Vespa.

'Can I drop you somewhere?' she asked.

'No, I have got my . . . Yes . . . actually you could.' Radhika narrowed her eyes at him and he hoped she hadn't figured out his ruse to spend more time with her.

'Look at that! People don't even know how to park their cars. Ridiculous!' she yelled, on seeing a car parked in front of her office building, blocking her scooter. 'They have cars but no brains.'

Funnily enough, it was Madhav's car but he played along.

'The guy who parked this way must be so stupid. Couldn't he see he was blocking my scooter?'

'You are right. Such people should die,' said Madhav, vehemently.

'No, they should not die. They should be punished,' Radhika said and gave him a roguish smile.

'What do you mean?' he asked as she handed him her helmet and sat on her haunches. Before he could say or do anything, he heard the sound of a tyre deflating.

'Oh God! Stop it, Radhika! For God's sake,' he screamed, forgetting his act for a second.

She looked up. 'Why are you screaming?'

'I mean, it's not fair!' He gnashed his teeth, trying to hide his annoyance.

She let out the last bit of air and then they struggled to pull her scooter out. Madhav sat behind her.

She started her Vespa and he smiled at her in the side-view mirror. She got the feeling that he hadn't smiled quite this much in a while and felt glad that he was happy around her.

'Where do you want me to drop you?'

'Wherever you want.'

'Huh?'

'I mean, you could drop me off at the University metro station,' he said as they drove off. He wanted to hold her waist but gripped her shoulders instead, not wanting to be too forward. The cool breeze whipped their hair. Her fragrance intoxicated him and their proximity made him acutely aware of every passing second.

'Why are there no speed breakers?' he muttered under his breath.

'What?'

'Nothing!'

Radhika dropped him off at the station. 'See you soon. And Madhav, I had a great time with you!'

'Me too. Well, wish me luck!' he said.

'For what?'

'I have an interview the day after tomorrow.'

'A corporate job?' He nodded. She made a face. 'Ugh! I shouldn't wish you luck so you can focus on your writing instead.' She shook his hand and sped off.

He smiled and stood looking at her until she disappeared amidst the cars. It had been one of the best days he'd had but this blissful haze was rudely interrupted by yet another call from Meera.

'Are you preparing for the interview? Hold on, I hear honking. Are you out?' She peppered him with questions.

'Meera! You are . . . My car is punctured. I'll call you back.'

He hopped on to a rickshaw to return to the office and called a mechanic to fix his car. He wasn't angry or annoyed. Rather, he was amused at Radhika's childish antics and thought of her even more fondly. For the first time in a long while, he felt like himself, light and free.

He reached home to a text from Radhika. *Thank you, Madhav. I haven't felt this happy in a long time. I hope no more rats commit suicide in your room.*

Madhav smiled and dropped on to his bed. His mother came upstairs to check on him and seeing him smile made her heart swell with joy again.

He began scribbling in his notebook and, this time, to his surprise, he wrote about embracing life instead of detesting it. It's incredible what a slight change of perspective or an interaction with a special soul can do.

Life has plenty of moments
When the path splits in two,
We'll walk in the dark
And if we stay together,
We will make it through.

5

Radhika dragged herself out of bed as the morning sunlight poured in through a gap in her bedroom curtains. She meditated, did her yoga, showered, blow-dried her hair and pulled the whole mess back into a ponytail. She put some moisturizer on her tattoo and dressed in her usual attire, a kurta and a pair of trousers. She then applied some mascara on to her lashes, dabbed on some cherry lip gloss and slipped on a pair of long peacock feather earrings and silver bangles. Radhika enjoyed breaking the conventional image of serious psychoanalysts.

She had been living by herself for four years now. She, too, harboured her own stories and secrets, some of which were probably as confounding as Madhav's.

Suresh, her programme manager, emailed her the weekly schedule that morning. She had multiple appointments booked—it was going to be a hectic week. But she was still perplexed by Madhav's case. She did not know his earlier diagnoses but felt quite invested in him already. She hadn't received any calls or messages from him for the past two days, despite his eagerness to see her again. She was concerned and thought about texting him when her phone beeped. It was Madhav. She smiled at the universe's sense of humour.

'*Ms Analyst, I too am an analyst now. I got the job! Business Analyst at Emarket.*' Radhika smiled and shook her head.

'*I think you are my lucky charm.*' He texted again.

'*But I didn't even wish you luck,*' she replied, dumping a load of clothes into the washing machine.

'*Your presence was lucky enough.*' A straight drive for four runs! Radhika blushed.

'*So where are we meeting for the party?*' he asked. She was a bit worried that he was falling for her. She loved his gestures and company but was too cautious to succumb to it. She knew Madhav was only attracted to her because of the forced intimacy of their relationship.

'*No, Madhav. I'm busy with appointments today,*' she replied. Madhav didn't respond, which made Radhika restless. She wanted to see him, but was afraid she would fall for him. She didn't want him to develop feelings for her either. He was a young man, exploring his life and confronting the demons of his past, while she was a twenty-nine-year-old psychoanalyst, who had her own struggles with the past.

Nevertheless, she checked her inbox obsessively, unable to reason with her edginess. She made her morning tea and toast. Sitting on her new red beanbag, she tried to distract herself by reading the newspaper but all her attention was on her phone.

She finally picked it up and with a piece of toast between her teeth, dialled Madhav's number. He disconnected the call. She tried again and again, but he didn't answer. Radhika gave up and decided to focus on work instead, berating herself for behaving like a teenager.

~

Later that morning, Madhav went to Meera's place, Skyhigh Estates, a luxurious apartment situated on the outskirts of Delhi. As soon as he entered her apartment, she jumped off the bed and leapt into his arms. Before he could tell her about the job, she began kissing his neck. Madhav tried to pull away but she started unbuttoning his shirt. He pushed her away gently as she took off her top.

'Please, Meera. Not now,' he said, firmly. She was taken aback as he was usually the one who would initiate sex. She put her top back on and drew open the curtains.

'Meera, I got the job!' he said. She turned to him with a big fake smile plastered on her face and ran into his arms.

'I knew it! I knew it! You're my rock star!' she screamed. 'Finally! You have to take me shopping now!'

Asking himself why he was even with her, Madhav had to admit that the only reason they were together was purely because of the physical satisfaction they derived from each other.

She would call him over on days when her flatmate wasn't around. But that morning, he didn't even want to touch her. All his thoughts were preoccupied with Radhika. He was caught between lust and love that morning and he instinctively chose love. He had been experiencing a sense of relief ever since he met her. He finally felt as if he was one person, instead of two.

'My baby wants wild sex tonight?' Meera asked, as she ran a finger down his inner thigh.

'Stop it, Meera!' he said, irritated. Meera was annoyed and sat down at her study table, sulking.

'Can't we just sit and talk instead, Meera?' he asked.

'Oh really, Madhav? You want to talk? I thought you only wanted sex all the time,' she said, as she opened a book and pretended to read. 'You know, I need to think about my future, too, but that's never occurred to you. I always support you and you've never even been thankful,' she said.

He laughed scornfully. He knew she just wanted to eat and shop on his dime. He also knew that she had lost all interest in pursuing management studies or any career, for that matter. He was only grateful to her for one thing, for taking him to the art therapy workshop.

'Good, I'm glad you've come to your senses. You should focus on your studies. See you later!' Madhav buttoned up his shirt and picked up his keys from the table, but Meera clutched his hand in desperation.

'Madhav, sorry, baby! I was just excited about your job. Don't I deserve to be happy?'

He pulled his hand away, lit a cigarette and checked his phone to see if Radhika had texted.

'Are we staying in tonight? Richa is out all night. Let's have some wine and we can talk to your heart's content,' she said. What a bimbo, thought Madhav.

'Okay, Meera, we'll see. I need to go home now to tell my mom about the job,' he said, putting out the cigarette on an ashtray. She stood up and kissed his cheek and was worried when he didn't reciprocate.

By the time he reached home, it was afternoon, which was the best time for him since his annoying sister and father would be at work and his mother would usually be at a relative's place.

But that day was different. Sauntering in, he saw everyone in the living room. He realized that he kind of missed spending time with his family. For the past twelve years, ever since he had returned from Nainital, he had avoided conversing with them. They deeply cared about Madhav, but he was wary about spending too much time with them.

'Madhav, is everything okay?' his mother asked.

His dad looked at him, unsmilingly, while Vihana chattered away on the phone.

'Didn't you have an interview yesterday? You didn't tell us how it went. What happened?' His mother fired her questions at him in one breath, which usually irked him, but to everyone's surprise, he smiled.

'I got the job,' he said. His father smiled and congratulated him in his surly yet proud way, while his mother caressed his cheeks. Vihana hung up and said, 'Good job, dude!' and patted his shoulder. 'Well, we have good news for you as well,' she added.

'What?'

'We've fixed a date for Vihana's wedding,' said his father.

Madhav beamed. 'Wow! You and Karan are getting married?' he asked. Vihana blushed and nodded. It had been many years since they had all been in one room this way, smiling and talking. His mother teared up at his reaction.

Madhav hugged Vihana. Life hadn't allowed them too many such moments. 'Congrats! I am so happy. I know you love him because you can never stop talking to him!' he teased her.

Madhav could feel something transforming within him, slowly but steadily. He knew it was because of Radhika and suddenly he ached to see her again.

~

Madhav bought flowers and pastries on the way to her office, dabbing cologne on his neck as he parked the car, far away from her scooter this time.

He climbed the stairs to her office but found the door closed. He rang the cowbell multiple times and eventually heard footsteps. It was around 6 p.m. Suresh opened the door.

'Suresh!' Madhav greeted him in surprise, trying in vain to hide the box of pastries and the flowers.

'Madhav!' Suresh looked at him warily.

'Is Radhika here?' Madhav asked as Suresh glanced at the bouquet and the pastry box out of the corner of his eye.

'She is not here. She's gone to visit a client,' Suresh said.

'When will she be back?'

'I don't know, but I'm closing the office in an hour. The door to her house is on the other side of the staircase.'

'Oh, okay. I guess I should leave.'

'How are you doing?' Suresh asked, in his usual drawl.

'I'm good.'

'Is it someone's birthday?' he inquired.

'No, uh, these are nothing . . . just like that. I'll leave then.'

Madhav was slightly upset as he'd desperately wanted to see Radhika again. He left in a hurry and drove back to his place. His mind was spinning and, in his anger, he switched off his phone. He stopped at a wine and beer shop and bought a bottle of Jack Daniel's, which he opened immediately, taking two long sips. He had planned on spending this evening celebrating with Radhika, but all his plans had gone awry. He drove recklessly and parked his car on the road, uncaring of the traffic.

He then went up to his room, ignoring everyone.
They were taken aback to see this behaviour after the
afternoon's pleasantries.

Up in his room, Madhav poured some more
whiskey into a glass and put on his headphones. But
after a minute or two, he took it off and staggered to
the mirror.

He stood there for a couple of minutes, looking
at every curve on his face. He went as close as he
possibly could, running a finger down his cheek in his
reflection.

'Isn't this what you've always wanted? An MBA
degree, a gold medal and a corporate job?' His eyes had
turned red.

'Tell me? Is there anything else you want? Anything
else you want to make me do?' He bit his lips, trying to
control his tears. His lips quivered as he once again felt
the familiar war within his mind and soul.

He grinned and grimaced through his tears. It was the
most frightening sight.

'This is not enough!' he yelled at himself. 'This is
not enough, Madhav. You have more debts to pay.'
And he laughed. He went into mad paroxysms of
laughter and then he started to sob. Anyone looking at
him would've thought him to be insane, but Madhav
didn't care because his true tormenter resided within
him.

His phoned beeped. It was Meera. His vision
went blurry as the three pegs of whiskey hit him all at
once.

'*I thought you would come over. I even bought a bottle of red wine to celebrate your success, but I guess you took the cake and roses to the wrong address. Don't call me ever again!*'

6

Madhav woke up at 7 a.m. He was on the floor with drool all over his face. His limbs ached but nothing seemed to be broken. His mouth tasted like something had died in there.

He shook his head and blinked rapidly to regain his focus. He got up in a hurry to check his phone but found that the screen was blank. He quickly plugged his charger in. He tried to recollect the events of the previous evening. All he could remember was reading Meera's message about him taking the pastries and bouquet to the wrong place. But how could she possibly have known that?

He ran downstairs and checked his car only to find that he had indeed forgotten his gifts at Radhika's office. He came back upstairs and switched on his phone, which immediately started buzzing with unread messages.

'*I am sorry, Madhav. I was with a client. I tried calling but your phone was switched off,*' Radhika had texted him, followed by, '*Goodnight. Take care.*'

He scrolled down. Meera had sent two messages. The second one was '*Fuck you!*'

The first said, '*I never thought you would cheat on me!*'

Madhav was relieved that Meera was finally breaking up with him, but was still perplexed at how she'd found out about his trip to Radhika's office.

He sat cross-legged on the swing in his terrace and was about to dial Meera's number when he saw that there were a few more messages from her.

'*Don't you dare call me, Madhav. I don't want to see you ever again.*'

'*I know I will never have any clarity on this because of your pride, but I loved you.*'

Madhav called her. She didn't answer but called him back in a minute.

'How dare you call me?' she bellowed.

'Why did you call me back?' he replied.

'Because I'm courteous.'

'Can we meet tonight?' he asked. He wanted to talk to her about his feelings for Radhika.

'No way in hell! Why did you go to her office with a bouquet and a box of pastries? Are you cheating on me?' she asked, nearly hysterical.

'Radhika, just listen to me,' he said.

'Radhika? You called me Radhika?' she screamed.

'Shit! Shit! Shit!' he mumbled and pressed his throbbing temples.

'Enough, Madhav! That's enough. I care for you, I do everything for you and this is how you treat me?' she sounded as though she was on the verge of tears.

Madhav stayed quiet for a while before asking her one last time, 'Do you want to meet me and talk about it?' She hung up on him.

His phone beeped almost instantly. It was a message from Meera.

'*9 p.m., my place.*'

She was under the impression that he would apologize profusely and admit it was only she whom he loved but, of course, the truth is usually more caustic than we expect.

Madhav didn't call or text Radhika the entire day.

~

Madhav reached Meera's place and parked his grey Honda City in her private parking space. Her flatmate worked at a call centre and had the night shift several times a week, so Meera often had the apartment to herself. He usually came over on those nights, but this particular visit was significantly different.

The young security guard, who had noticed Madhav's frequent visits, faked a big smile as Madhav got out of his car with a bag full of beer, Scotch and cans of soda.

'Hello sir! How are you?' The guard followed him, hoping for a tip.

Madhav stopped. As he pulled out his wallet, two condoms fell out. The guard's eyes widened. Madhav immediately handed him a five-hundred-rupee note. The young boy smiled wickedly and ran back to his post.

Madhav picked up the condoms and threw them in the bushes. He didn't intend to use them that night.

He entered the lift and combed his fingers through his hair, exhaling into his cupped palm to check his breath. The lift smoothly sailed upwards and stopped at the thirteenth floor.

He rang the doorbell. Nobody opened the door. He rang it again but there was still no response. He dialled Meera's number but found that it was switched off. Perhaps she had changed her mind about talking to him, he thought. There was a beeping sound from the elevator lobby as one of the lifts opened. Meera stepped out. She wore a dress shorter than Madhav's temper along with a pearl necklace and high heels. Her hair was sleeker and shinier than ever, but it was her musky perfume that bowled Madhav over as she walked towards him. Her velvet eyelashes beckoned him closer.

'Where were you?' he asked. She hugged him and replied, 'Didn't I tell you that I had gone to the parlour?'

'I received the payment alert!'

She grasped his collar gently and pulled him into the apartment, behaving as though nothing had happened. But Madhav was not going to fall for her seductive act. She tried to arouse him by gently scratching him with her crimson fingernails, and shoved him towards the couch. Madhav dropped his bag on the floor and held her waist.

'What do you want from me tonight?' She leaned forward to kiss him.

'To kill you,' he said, suddenly incensed. His thoughts and emotions were bubbling up inside him again, but this time they were compelled by a dark rage. He tried to suppress it and control himself but he was slowly losing his grip.

Meera laughed gaily, forgetting the severity of his mood swings.

'I always knew you were a killer,' she said unthinkingly, oblivious to Madhav's rising anger. Her reply pierced through him, to the heart of all his nightmares and secrets. His memories came rushing back to him.

'What did you say?' Madhav's ears turned red as he grabbed her roughly.

'Madhav, what are you doing?' Meera was starting to get scared.

'You think I am a killer? You think . . .' he mumbled and held her jaw tightly, forcing her face upwards. Petrified, Meera tried to push him away but his hold on her was stronger than ever.

'Maddy, you're hurting me. Please let me go,' she pleaded.

'I *will* hurt you. I am a killer, aren't I?' he started losing control as anger overpowered all his other emotions.

'I am sorry, Maddy,' Meera cried.

'I should kill you before you tell anyone else,' he snarled as drops of sweat dripped down his face.

'Maddy, what are you talking about? Please calm down.' She begged him to stop. And to her surprise, he did. The abrupt shift in Madhav's behaviour was extremely unnerving. He was maniacal one minute and completely Zen-like the next. But Meera had not seen the worst; even Madhav wasn't sure what he was capable of doing during one of his fits.

He sat down on the couch as Meera adjusted her dress with trembling hands. She breathed heavily and sat down next to him. Madhav emptied his bag, smiling, as though nothing had happened. Meera stared at him in disbelief for a couple of minutes, too afraid to voice her fear. She had seen him rage against the students at college before suddenly calming down just like he had right now, but she had never borne the brunt of it herself.

'Get the glasses,' he ordered. Still unsure of how to react and scared that he might get angry, she got up and slowly walked towards the home bar.

'Who told you about the bouquet and the pastries?' he asked, chugging a beer.

'Suresh called me,' she murmured, still scared.

'Why did he call you?'

'He said you'd come to meet Radhika and had forgotten the box and bouquet there,' she said as she handed him a glass. 'He tried calling you but your phone was switched off.'

Madhav shook his head as he finished off a pint of Fosters. 'So he called to ask if you were with me,' she explained nervously.

There was a moment of silence. 'Why did you go to her house with flowers and pastries?' she asked.

'Because I wanted to.' Madhav opened another bottle of beer with his teeth.

He picked up her guitar and went to the balcony. She took the glasses and followed him outside. She was still in shock and moved as though she had little control over her actions. Madhav began playing the guitar, singing a Bryan Adams song. His voice was calm. Meera felt relaxed.

The view from the balcony was mesmerizing. The world looked miniscule and distant. The lights from cars and buildings pulsed like LEDs on a giant switchboard. They sat in the dark, the balcony illuminated with the faint light from the drawing room.

'Madhav, I want you to see a good therapist,' she said, holding his arm and kissing his bicep.

Madhav stopped playing the guitar. 'What? Why?' He placed the instrument aside and lit a cigarette.

'I just think you need to see a proper psychiatrist. Your mood swings are starting to scare me, to be honest, and I don't think some bullshit art therapy will give you the help you need. Especially with that bitch Radhika and her phoney nonsense.' Meera held him tighter. She couldn't help sounding jealous of his obsession with Radhika, but she also felt a bit awkward voicing her concerns so directly to him. During the five months of their relationship, she had seen many of his scary moods, but little did she know that her words would release a monster within him, a dark and unfathomable beast.

Madhav's head began aching severely and blood thundered in his ears. He blew a puff of smoke in Meera's face. She coughed and pushed him away. He chuckled at her discomfort.

'Are you crazy?' she asked. He blew another puff in her direction and the smoke obscured her face. She started coughing even harder, but he did not care.

'Madhav, stop it!' she screamed in desperation. His desire and anger bled into one another. He held her chin roughly and, forcing open her mouth, exhaled smoke directly into it. Meera cried for help, even though she knew no one could hear her.

'What are you doing, dammit?' she screamed. She snatched the cigarette from his hand and threw it down from the balcony. Madhav's eyes followed the arc of the falling cigarette.

'Madhav, please let me go,' Meera pleaded.

He held her arms so tightly that they went numb. 'What do you want from me?' he asked, looking into her eyes. His voice had a strange frightening edge to it. Her eyes widened.

'Do you think I am mad? Do you think I need a doctor? Do you think Radhika is a bitch?' He repeated these questions, louder and louder. It was as though they were powering his anger. Meera was frozen in fear. She couldn't understand how her concern had precipitated such a reaction. She was also unaware of the strength of his feelings for Radhika.

'How dare you call her a bitch, you ignorant slut!' His voice cracked under the strain. 'You've gone too far now. Tonight I will show you who the bitch really is,' he said. 'You are a cheater! You are a cheater!'

He was mad! Meera couldn't make out what he was trying to do. His actions and words changed every second.

He looked like a victim and a criminal at the same time. It was as if he was angrier with himself than with Meera. He wanted to hurt himself.

'What are you saying?' She struggled to push him away from her. He held her from behind. She struggled to break free. He held on tighter, not brutally but as if to seek help, as if someone was hurting him.

He pulled her hair as she screamed out loud. He could feel the darkness swirling around in his mind.

'You will call her and apologize, you bitch!' he said. He was completely lost in an abyss.

Suddenly, he began howling. 'I am sorry, Meera. I am really sorry,' he said. 'I love Radhika. I could never love you that way.' Then he felt his limbs starting to give way. 'I can't feel my legs. I cannot move,' he said, panicking. Meera took advantage of his sudden weakness and picked up a bottle, bringing it down on his head. The bottle didn't break since she didn't smash it hard enough. But it debilitated him and he crashed on to the floor, wheezing, his head throbbing unbearably.

'Now I will show you who I am, Madhav Mehra. You will suffer for calling me a bitch!'

Pain and alcohol took over his senses and he passed out.

7

Madhav woke up from a dream where he was struggling to breathe underwater, to find his nose blocked with dried blood from when he fell to the floor the previous night. He was still in Meera's apartment. He didn't remember most of the night, as always, but he could tell something horrific had happened. There was a strange silence in the apartment as though it had been quarantined. Beer bottles, half-smoked cigarettes and joints were strewn across the room.

'Meera,' he whispered, as he stood up, body and head aching badly. He was tired of waking up like this every morning. He went to the bathroom, peeked in all the bedrooms and the kitchen but couldn't find anyone.

He had flashbacks of mistreating Meera, but couldn't remember what he'd done to her. He remembered her calling Radhika a bitch and then his memory failed him. He could only remember anger and darkness.

Madhav sat on the couch, his head in his hands. He had an absurd feeling—as though he were impersonating himself or living in a vicious loop of his own making. He tried to jog his memory, nearly hitting himself in frustration. Images of Meera screaming and trying to push him away flashed in his mind.

He looked around for his phone and finally found it under one of the couch cushions. There were no messages or calls. As he was about to dial Meera's number, there was a loud thump against the door. The pounding continued as he hid his stash of hash under the couch and walked to the door. He took one deep breath and opened it. There were two men in police uniforms, glowering at him. Before he could comprehend the situation, one of the men who had a grand moustache asked, 'Madhav Mehra?'

Madhav nodded, petrified, thousands of possibilities buzzing in his aching head.

'But this is not my home,' he murmured.

'We know, young man. The problem is that this is not your home,' he said, gruffly.

'Problem? But this is my friend's home,' Madhav said, trying to regain some semblance of confidence.

'This "friend" has filed a sexual harassment and attempt to rape complaint against you,' the man said.

'Sir . . . listen to me. It's not like that. I mean, I don't remember.' He pleaded as both the policemen gripped him firmly by the shoulders and warned him, 'If you resist, we will drag you to the car.'

Shocked by this turn of events, he went and sat quietly in the car. He again racked his brain, trying to recollect the night's events but he couldn't remember a thing. He thought of calling Radhika, and even though he was terrified of what she would think once she heard about his state, he didn't want to talk to anyone else. When she picked up, he told her about his rage blackout and the sexual assault charges Meera had pressed. He remembered mistreating her but he had no memory of sexual harassment or rape. He told Radhika that Meera's charges were false. But before he could give her any other details, the head constable took away his phone. The policemen got into the car and drove towards the police station.

As he entered the station, Madhav saw a slim figure near the front desk.

'Meera?' he uttered in surprise. She refused to look at him.

A senior officer called them into his office and asked everyone to sit. Madhav stood motionless. They didn't handcuff or beat him; they only surrounded him with grim looks on their faces.

'Yes, madam, tell me,' the senior officer said. He had a dignified and firm voice. His badge read Mahavir Singh and he was the station house officer.

Before Meera could speak, a lady constable said to the SHO, 'Please see the report, sir. She has not filed an FIR yet.'

'Ms Meera,' the officer adjusted his glasses and continued, 'you have reported an incident of molestation. Mr Madhav broke into your house and forcefully ill-treated you and when you objected to his behaviour, he became angry and sexually abused you and even attempted to rape you.'

Meera nodded, her eyes brimming with tears. 'Broke into the house? Rape?' Madhav repeated. 'Meera, why are you doing this?'

'Because of what you did last night,' she said, still refusing to look at him.

'But I don't remember anything. The last thing I remember is coming over,' he said.

'Don't worry, we will get it out of you,' the inspector said with a menacing expression.

Meera's phone rang and she excused herself. The atmosphere in the room immediately became tenser as the officers glared at him. Madhav counted the minutes until Meera returned.

She had left the room to answer a call from an unknown number. 'Hello, who's this?' she asked.

'It's Radhika.'

'Why the hell are you calling me? I don't want to talk to you.'

'Meera, wait! Just hear me out for a minute,' Radhika pleaded with her. She knew it was a difficult time for her, but she had to try for Madhav's sake.

'I don't want to listen to anything. I cannot take his insanity any more.'

'He needs to get proper help for his issues. If you file a false case, things will only get worse for him and his family. Please just give him a chance to get better; you don't have to deal with his problems any more. I promise I'll help him.'

'Oh yes, of course! That's what you want, Radhika. You want me to leave him so you can have him all to yourself. Don't worry. I am leaving him and I bet you will also leave this sick man in no time. I shouldn't have taken him to your crappy art therapy class. But I refuse to let him go unpunished.'

'I know what happened was absolutely unacceptable, and that he should be punished. But the thing is, he is already being punished every day. He says he doesn't remember anything and I know he is not lying,' Radhika said. 'You know the truth, Meera. Only you know if he actually tried to rape you. I would simply request you to drop the charges if they are false. If Madhav did sexually abuse you, I promise you that I will stand by you and together we will make sure that he is punished. But if he's innocent, then I want you to come forward and save him because he is already suffering. I leave the decision to you.'

Her words hit Meera but she was not one to accept defeat easily.

'Oh really? You're trying to question my conscience now? You seem to have got to know him very well in just a few days.' Meera laughed humourlessly at her, though she knew what she was doing was wrong.

'I don't know him, Meera, but I want to know him. I know he is going through something deeply troubling,' Radhika said.

'Look, Radhika. Maybe I am not as great a person as you are. I wanted to be valued but he never did that. I can't bear it any longer. I just wish both of you a great life.'

'Wait . . . wait! I don't have any feelings for him and I am sure Madhav doesn't have feelings for me either.

We just share a formal relationship and I care for him because he's my patient,' Radhika tried to clarify.

'Really? You should know that everything that happened last night was because I insulted you. He lied to me about visiting your office and then mistreated me because I called you a bitch. He has lost his senses because of you and you're claiming it's a platonic relationship? He said he loves you.'

'What? Why would he lie to you? Why would he say that he loves me? And why would he do all that to you because of me?' Radhika sounded stunned and perplexed.

'Why don't you ask Madhav what he did?'

Radhika was left dumbfounded. Madhav had truly fallen for her and she would now have to face the consequences head-on.

Meera disconnected the call and returned to the SHO's office. She said, 'I am sorry, sir. But I want to solve this matter personally.'

Everyone looked surprised and the SHO said, 'This is not acceptable, madam. You are not allowed to waste our time like this.'

'I am sorry, sir,' she said and abruptly walked out. Madhav was flabbergasted. What had happened in the last few minutes to change Meera's mind?

'She spared you this time,' the inspector said and asked him to leave. 'But if you repeat this, no one will save you.' He turned to his men. 'This generation has no consideration for people's time. They get into trouble, complain and then step back. Then they say the police doesn't help!' the SHO muttered grumpily as Madhav walked out after Meera.

'Meera! Please stop!' She looked back at him and said, 'Madhav, I just have one thing to say to you. I will never see you again. I may not have loved you but I didn't deserve this.'

Meera walked off and Madhav did not stop her this time. He felt guilty for the pain he had caused her and wanted to apologize for it, but he didn't know what he could say to make things better. So he let her go. He knew it would be good for both of them. But that didn't stop him from cursing himself for what he had done, even if he couldn't remember it.

~

Radhika knew that in order to address Madhav's deep-seated issues, she had to be as normal as possible with him, despite all that had happened.

'Hello,' Madhav's voice trembled as he answered her call.

'Madhav, are you free to speak to me?' Radhika asked, in a low, soothing voice. He was still in shock from the day's events. He couldn't believe that he had actually assaulted Meera simply because she had insulted Radhika. What had he become? He tried to push away the overwhelming despair knocking at his mind's door.

'Yes.'

'I am going to ask you a couple of questions and it's up to you whether you want to answer them or not. Are you fine with that?' Radhika's words were as serene as gentle waves.

'Yes,' Madhav mumbled in agreement.

He was sitting locked up in his room. His family had no idea what had happened or what he was going through. He was far too ashamed and scared to tell them.

'Madhav, what exactly do you remember from last night?' Radhika asked.

He exhaled shakily. 'I clearly remember buying alcohol from the wine and beer shop and then driving to Meera's apartment. She was upset that I had come to your place after I got the job. I went over to her place to apologize and tell her that I didn't want to be with her.' He paused.

'She wanted to get physical. I felt a strange urge and I admit I became violent. I remember being quite shocked by my actions. But I soon calmed down and started playing the guitar. I hardly recollect anything between then and when she hit me. I did not force myself on her, Radhika. I would never do that.'

Radhika noted down the key points. His behavioural patterns were unconventional and did not clearly suggest any particular root cause. She had dealt with patients suffering from depression before but his case was more complex.

'We were drinking on the balcony and she provoked me by saying I need psychiatric help, after which we argued about you. I tried to stop myself from getting angry again, but then she called you a bitch and I honestly don't remember what happened next. I think I lost control of my senses. It was as if I had been ripped apart from my body and something else took over. I could sense something terrible happening but I felt caged and helpless in the face of this force.' Madhav was shaking, sweat forming on his brow. He sank into his couch and tried to breathe normally.

'It's okay, Madhav. It's fine.' Radhika tried to channel his thoughts and emotions before they consumed him. She had conducted several such sessions recently, but never had any of them touched her so deeply. She had known her relationship with Madhav wasn't going to be like those with other patients when she saw his painting.

'It wasn't me who mistreated Meera, it wasn't me! It was that voice, that spirit that overtook my body. I wasn't in control, I swear . . . You have to believe me, Radhika. I didn't want to hurt her!' Madhav broke down as he tried to explain his torment in a way that he never had to anyone else, not even to himself. She recorded everything. She felt an inexplicable tenderness towards him.

'I understand, Madhav. I just want you to sleep well tonight and I will help you work through this. I am here for you,' she assured him.

'Will you always be there for me?' he half-whispered. Silence filled the space between them for a few seconds. They could only hear each other breathing.

'Yes, Madhav. I will always be there,' she said, realizing that despite saying the same thing to many other patients, she had never meant it in quite this way.

8

Madhav stood in front of the mirror staring at his image, as he did every morning. He noticed each curve of his face and stared deep into his eyes. Crumpled sheets of poetry that he'd attempted to write the previous night lay scattered around him. His formal clothes stifled him—the noose-like tie, the too-tight belt. It was his first day at work. He stared at his image helplessly.

'Your dreams are coming true,' he spat at the mirror. He closed his eyes and stepped back.

His phone rang. 'Good morning, Madhav!' said Radhika.

'Good morning!' he replied, his tone suiting his attire.

'All set for the new day?' she asked. She was making breakfast, the phone tucked in the crook of her neck.

'Sort of. I mean it's pretty strange. I've worked hard for this but it feels quite empty now that I finally have it,' he said.

'That's because for you fulfilment lies in writing,' Radhika said.

'Well, I can see my words crushed, in the dustbin.'

'Madhav, you need to have faith in your abilities. Mark my words. These crushed scraps of paper will make a great book one day.' She poured herself a glass of milk.

'Are you having breakfast?' he asked.

'Yes. My breakfast is just a slice of toast, milk and cereal.'

'Lucky you! My mother is waiting downstairs with her oily aloo paranthas,' he said and chuckled a bit.

They had grown increasingly comfortable with one another and the length of their phone calls now stretched from minutes to hours. They would call each other first thing in the morning and last thing at night. Madhav knew Radhika had convinced Meera to not press charges against him and he was more in love with her than ever, but he still doubted if she had feelings for him.

'When are you inviting me over?' he asked.

'Ahem!' She cleared her throat. 'Yes, your sessions are pending. But make an appointment this time and please, no pastries.'

Both of them laughed and she wished him luck for his first day at work.

As he went downstairs, his mother greeted him with a bowl of curd and sugar. 'You look so handsome,' she said.

'Curd in the morning?'

'It's lucky, son,' she insisted.

'How can curd and sugar be lucky?' He considered arguing against it but gave in instead.

'Your dad and Vihana wished you luck,' his mother said and put a plate of aloo paranthas on the table. Madhav looked at his watch. He was told to report at 9 a.m.

'Ma, please pack my breakfast. I am running very late.'

'But we earn so we may eat peacefully. Food that is not eaten with love isn't worth eating at all. Tell me, what's the point in working so hard?'

'There's more to life than just food,' he retorted.

Madhav was a bit nervous as he drove to his new office. It seemed like a paradigm shift, from college to office. He would have to wear uncomfortable clothes and mind his language and behaviour. It all seemed extremely daunting. He tuned into his favourite FM channel and his thoughts wandered to what he had done to Meera. While he waited at a traffic signal, a beggar in a wheelchair knocked on his window. Madhav's heart skipped a beat as he stared at the wheelchair. He swallowed hard and sped off the second the light turned green.

His firm, Emarket, was a branding company situated in an imposing monolith. Madhav entered his details at the reception and went to the lift lobby. He saw a few really pretty, petite girls, dressed in formals, shooting him interested looks, but he only had Radhika on his mind. The lift stopped at the eighth floor.

A beautiful woman sat at the front desk. 'Hello, how may I help you?' she asked, flashing him a well-trained, fake smile.

'Hello! I am Madhav Mehra. I'm a new employee. I was asked to report to Mr Rao.'

'Let me call him.' She dialled a number and asked an HR executive about Madhav.

'You can go in and ask for Mr Rao,' said the receptionist. 'Welcome to Emarket.'

Madhav walked in and entered a huge space, with hundreds of symmetrical cubicles. It looked like a maze to him, a puzzle of sorts. He saw a man walking hurriedly towards the door and stopped him.

'Do you know Mr Rao?' he asked. The man looked very tense.

'I am going to his cabin. Come with me,' he said as he took off at a slow jog.

'Why are you walking so fast?' Madhav ran behind him.

'Mr Rao is strict about time and despises latecomers.'

Madhav looked at his watch. It was 9.45 a.m. He was already forty-five minutes late. They reached a cabin where the name on the door said, 'Vinesh Rao, Senior Manager, Analytics'.

'Sir, may I come in?' the man asked, trying to catch his breath. As Madhav peeped into the room, he saw a man in a white shirt rifling through papers.

Mr Rao scolded the man for sending in the reports late and asked him to redo all of them. Madhav waited for his turn. He finally called him in ten minutes later. A pair of glasses was perched on his nose and there were files strewn across his table.

'My name is Madhav Mehra,' he mumbled.

The man looked at the watch and then at Madhav.

'You are fifty-two minutes and forty-six seconds late, Mr Mehra,' he proclaimed.

'Sir, I am sorry. I got stuck in traffic,' Madhav said.

'I leave at seven every morning and reach either on or before time even if there's traffic. The problem with your generation is that you follow Google Maps blindly. You see the estimated time and then decide when to leave.' He laughed unexpectedly.

'Yes, sir,' Madhav said, shamefacedly.

'Oh! So you are one of them. Well, I don't have much time to spend on you. Go to the analytics wing and talk to your project manager.'

Madhav was surprised to be let off so easily and said a profuse 'Thank you.'

His project manager was an amiable guy who seemed to be around the same age as him.

Madhav shook hands with the guy, sizing him up. Maybe this was Mr Rao's model employee—well-dressed and polite, he looked like he was always early to arrive for everything.

'Hi! I'm Vipin, your project manager.'

'Nice to meet you, sir.'

'Same here but tough luck, man!' he said.

'Why is that, sir?'

'Vinesh has marked you absent on your first day!'

'Oh fuck!' Madhav muttered.

'He has also assigned you three modules,' Vipin added.

'When does he need them?' he asked.

'Today,' Vipin said apologetically as he handed him a stack of papers. Madhav took the heavy binders, already feeling suffocated. His first day at office had started off as a disaster. He was given a cubicle in a corner and assigned a shared computer.

'You may start now,' Vipin told him. 'There's a tea break at eleven, lunch at two, another break at five and you can leave once you've completed your tasks for the day.'

Madhav could foresee the robotic life he was going to lead. Each minute in the office choked him, smothered his dreams and stifled his happiness. He sighed and looked at the modules. He didn't know what he was doing there or why he had studied so hard only to achieve this. Maybe he didn't want to admit it to himself or tell anyone. It was a deep secret that had led him there.

The entire day passed in a blur. He didn't even have time for lunch or to reply to Radhika's texts because he was so burdened with work.

He opened his lunch box only at seven in the evening. He looked around the almost empty office. Lights were being switched off one by one and he was yet to start on the last module. But he had promised to meet Radhika. He peeked in Vinesh's cabin. He was intently working.

'Sir, I need to visit my doctor. I have finished two modules,' he said as politely as he could as he placed the completed modules on his table.

'Which doctor?' Vinesh asked, flipping through the files.

'My dentist,' Madhav lied.

'Cancel your appointment. The client needs all three modules today.' Vinesh pointed him to the door. Madhav was furious but he bit his tongue. And to think he'd been marked absent while he'd slaved away all day! He felt like yelling as he saw the office emptying out.

His phone beeped with a message from Radhika. '*Are we still on for tonight?*'

'*I am sorry. It's not possible,*' he replied. He ate the ice-cold paranthas while working on the final module. It was only once the employees on the night shift had started trickling in that Vinesh came to his cubicle and said, 'You may leave now. Hand over the module to one of your team members.'

Madhav was surprised to see Vinesh still in the office. He handed over the documents to a teammate who told him, 'Vinesh doesn't leave until eleven or so, and no matter how early you come in, he will be here before you. He basically lives in the office.'

It was ten by the time Madhav left. 'I won't even get a beer right now,' he muttered to himself. 'It's times like these that I miss Meera.' He checked his phone. Radhika had sent him a message. '*Call me when you get home.*'

His day had been completely fucked up. As he entered his house, he walked straight into his room, ignoring his mother's call for dinner. He immediately lit a cigarette and went out on to the terrace. He looked up at the stars and mulled over his day. He loosened his tie and called Radhika.

'Hello, Mr Analyst,' she teased, but he was in no mood for jokes and merely grunted in response.

'Someone's tired,' she said.

'What should I do, Radhika? I can't spend another day of my life in that place. They are all robots. They come in, they work, they eat, they work and then they leave. I can't have such a mind-numbing existence.'

'Then resign!' She chuckled.

'Come on! Please don't make fun of my situation.'

'Madhav, I love it when people have to face such situations in life. This is one of the most important phases in your life. You stand at a crossroads and you need to decide which direction your life should take. Only you can determine this. Nobody else.'

'But they're paying me well. How will I earn a living if I resign? I can't live on my dad's money forever,' Madhav said as he tossed the cigarette off the terrace. He went back into his room to undress, putting the call on speakerphone.

Radhika was painting while she talked to him, a nightly routine that helped her de-stress.

'They are not really paying you for your skill or your intellect, but for your time, which is priceless, Madhav. If you recognized the true worth of your time, you wouldn't spend it in the frivolous quest for money. Instead, you would spend it on what you love. If you write for a living, you might earn less, but you will go to sleep happy. There might be hunger in your stomach but not in your heart.' Radhika rambled on in her usual fashion.

'That's easier said than done.'

'No, Madhav. I know that if you continue working there, you will come back and crib about the routine every day and feel that your life is getting wasted,' she said. She fervently believed in doing work that came from the heart. But Madhav knew all this—he just couldn't overcome the voices that obstructed the path to his true passion.

'Why do you care so much about me?' He tried to ease the mood.

'I . . . because I am your analyst and it's my job!' she said.

Madhav smiled because he could hear the lack of conviction in her voice. She was trying to convince both him and herself.

'Okay, Ms Analyst. When is our next session?'

'Whenever you decide to leave this pathetic job!' Both of them smiled as they said goodnight.

Madhav felt strangely content; it was the first time he had felt something positive all day.

~

In the meantime, Radhika knew she had started developing feeling for Madhav. She tried to deny it by telling herself that it was just an interesting case, but somewhere deep in her heart she was growing increasingly attached to him.

That night, her painting was full of shades of orange and red. The warm pulse of love infused her mind and flowed through her limbs, manifesting in her painting. She tried to suppress it, but love cannot be suppressed. It doesn't let anyone escape its hold. She looked at her painting and felt both weird and wonderful at the same time.

She slept poorly that night. She kept thinking about Madhav. She was worried about his job, his issues, his mind. She got out of bed and wrote down the details of his case from the very beginning. She planned her sessions with him to begin untangling his problems and to help him heal. She knew she had to navigate her feelings very carefully. Being Madhav's therapist, she couldn't afford to behave unprofessionally.

But Radhika and Madhav grew closer each day. She would think of him even when she was with other patients, while he'd spend the entire day at work aching to talk to her. The universe had started weaving the silver thread of their beautiful relationship while they had no idea what lay in store for them.

9

31 December 2011

Days passed and nights rolled by. Madhav now grew accustomed to the daily grind of reporting to Vinesh and receiving a ton of work. He decided to finally catch up with Radhika during the weekend. The whole world would be stepping into a new year and Madhav hoped that the two of them would step into a new relationship. He called her early on Saturday morning.

'Where are we going?' she asked him.

'There's a New Year's Eve party at Kitty Su,' he said.

'Clubs are not my thing,' she shot back immediately.

'Then shall we meditate?'

'Yes. There couldn't be a better start to the New Year. Sitting with yourself and feeling the fresh morning air in your lungs. Ah!'

'Okay, how about this? We party at night and meditate in the morning. What do you say?' Madhav asked, feeling cocky.

103

'You are mad, Madhav!' She chuckled. 'We will meditate first,' she said.

'Can I say no?'

'No. See you in an hour.' Radhika smiled, having got her way.

They had made plans to meet earlier too, but Madhav always ended up getting stuck at the office. However, they spoke to each other every night. She could see an improvement in his behaviour as a result of their talks during which she would try to get him to open up and address his issues. He slowly began interacting with his family more often, making his mother very happy. He would always join them for dinner after work. She was very curious about the person who was engendering such a positive change in him. But he always deflected her questions.

After he hung up with Radhika, Madhav went downstairs and gave his mother a hug and asked, 'How are you, Mom?' He held her hand and sat on the sofa.

'Whom do you talk to at night on the phone?' she asked.

'Ma, come on! Not again.'

She saw him blush, which had never happened before.

'I'm guessing it isn't Meera,' she said.

'We do not talk any more and I don't want you to ask me any questions about it,' he said firmly.

'But then whom do you talk to?'

'Her name is Radhika. She is a friend. I mean, she's a therapist, but she's become a friend,' he said.

'You're going to meditate with her?' She had overheard snippets of his conversation.

'I don't know. I'll try.'

'Do you like her?'

'What are you saying, Ma?' He sounded exasperated, but smiled sheepishly as he left the room.

Madhav's mother was happy that her son was getting better. She wanted to meet Radhika but she knew she'd have to wait until he was ready.

~

Madhav and Radhika met at the gates of Raj Ghat. It was a bitterly cold and foggy morning. He wore a grey tracksuit while she was brightly attired in fuchsia.

'I'm surprised you haven't been to this peaceful place before,' she said.

'And I can't believe that I am going to meditate for an hour on my first visit,' he whined and made a face.

As Radhika chose a quiet space for them to sit, Madhav was struck by her simplicity and the will to help those around her relax and be happy. When she smiled and laughed, one couldn't help but smile as well. Her personality shone like the summer sun even on the gloomiest day.

'Okay, madam. Shall we start?' he asked.

'This hour of sunrise, nature's transition between day and night, will help calm our thoughts,' she said softly. Madhav squirmed at the thought of having to be spiritual.

She ignored him and continued, 'First, we need to sit in a comfortable position.'

She straightened her back and relaxed her shoulders. Madhav copied her movements.

'Now, we will close our eyes and take a few deep breaths.'

Madhav didn't close his eyes. He just wanted to observe Radhika—that was his idea of meditation. She looked serene and completely at peace, her hair flying gently in the wind.

'Smile a gentle smile,' she said. Madhav was held spellbound by her aura.

'Let go of all your frustrations. Feel them seeping out of you and into the ground with each measured breath.' She was quiet for a few minutes. Then she slowly opened her eyes to find Madhav gazing dreamily at her face.

'Madhav Mehra,' she said sternly, breaking his trance. He came back to his senses with a jerk.

'This is cheating,' she said.

'No, I just finished two minutes before you,' he lied.

'Hey, I know you pretty well by now, so don't try to fool me.' She stood up and brushed away the wet grass from her pants. 'There's no point trying to get you to meditate. We might as well leave,' she said.

'Are we going to the New Year's Eve party tonight as you promised?' Madhav asked as they walked back to the parking lot.

'Yes, we shall because you sort of held up your end of the deal,' she said as he made a puppy face.

'Be ready by eight,' he said as she sped off on her Vespa.

Radhika had asked Suresh to cancel all her appointments for the next two days. She was going to devote this time to helping Madhav.

Radhika looked at herself in the mirror. Despite her best efforts to curb them, her insecurities about her looks had intensified over the years. She refused to frequent clubs or parties with a young, hip crowd as she somehow felt inferior in their presence. Intellectually, she was aware that she was smart and capable, but she was unable to overcome her inherent insecurities about her appearance.

She looked through her wardrobe in search of a clubbing outfit. Her cupboard was full of kurtas and trousers. She wondered when she had become old and predictable. Falling in love or partying at a club wasn't her cup of tea. But when Madhav asked her out, she couldn't refuse. She picked up a glittery dress and looked for a pair of heels that she could wear with it. Suddenly frustrated, she threw the dress on her bed.

She picked up her phone and texted Madhav. '*I cannot go. I don't have anything appropriate to wear.*'

Madhav was desperately trying to finish his pending work, which had to be submitted on Monday morning.

He replied to her in a hurry. '*It will be dark in the club and no one will care. Just come!*'

Radhika smirked at his reply and searched for her best outfit. Even though she was an independent woman who was happy being by herself, it felt good to have someone who forced her to face her fear of opening up and trusting people.

That night, lights glittered in the streets and loud music blared out of the speakers set up for parties. Florists, bakeries and alcohol shops were packed with people stocking up on last-minute supplies.

Madhav put on a black jacket, jeans and ankle boots and went downstairs.

'Happy New Year,' he said to his parents who were in their cosy living room, watching an awards ceremony on television. He hugged them both, surprising them with his unexpected show of affection.

'Where's Vihana?' he asked.

'She has gone to a party at her friend's place,' his mother said. Madhav shook his head and said goodbye.

He spent the entire journey to Radhika's place anxiously checking his hair and face in the mirror. He honked as he reached her apartment building, but she didn't come out. He waited a while before calling her. But before her phone could ring, her apartment door opened. Madhav tried to peek at her through his car's rear-view mirror. She came out looking flawless. His jaw dropped. She wore a peacock-blue dress with a pearl necklace and long yet simple earrings that perfectly complemented her styled hair. Madhav was stunned. He realized that true beauty lay in how elegantly a woman could carry herself and wasn't determined by what she wore. And Radhika was the most elegant woman he had ever seen.

She walked slowly, her high heels clacking as she made her way to the car. Madhav got out to open the door for her. She paused and looked into his eyes. She had applied very little make-up—some mascara on her eyelashes and a matte red lipstick. She raised her eyebrows to wordlessly ask him how she looked. He gazed at her perfect glistening skin. His eyes were drawn to the string of pearls that gently caressed her neck, falling just below her collar bone. If the gods were real, he told himself, then this woman was their masterpiece.

'You've stolen my words,' he said and she laughed.

'I'm flattered,' she whispered. She loved how special he made her feel, a sensation she had quite forgotten. She felt inexplicably shy, as though she was once again a teenager on her first date.

'Wait, haven't I seen this car before?' she asked, as she scrutinized his Honda. 'It's the same one I punctured that day, isn't it?'

Madhav was taken aback. 'No, this is not the same car. I mean, the colour is different. That was a Honda City too but it was not grey,' he muttered.

'No, it's the exact same colour,' she exclaimed as she examined the car carefully. 'Madhav, tell me the truth,' she said, her eyes stern like a strict schoolteacher who could wrangle the truth out of you, no matter what.

'It's the same car,' he said, embarrassed.

Radhika laughed out loud. 'Oh my God! You are so scared of me that you saw me puncturing your tyres and didn't say anything. I simply can't believe it!' She ruffled his hair as he stood there sheepishly. She loved his naïve expression and he loved the way she caressed his head. They laughed about the incident until they reached the club, which was in one of Delhi's most luxurious hotels.

Madhav parked the car and as they walked towards the entrance, Radhika slipped her arm through his, which made him happy beyond measure. He gazed into her eyes and, for a moment, the sight of the two of them near the lit fountain looked like a scene from a rom-com.

'Shall we?' He took her hand and walked into the club. Radhika felt a familiar surge of anxiety as she wondered if she would fit in with the crowd, but was reassured when Madhav held her hand tightly as they climbed the dimly lit stairs.

There were over three hundred people dancing to incredibly loud music in the club. A few couples sat on couches, enjoying their drinks. There were single people at the bar, too, looking around for prospects to hit on as the night progressed. Madhav looked at Radhika closely as she ran her manicured hands, with fingernails painted red, through her brown hair. Her hair curled around her face and her swanlike neck.

'Gosh! I am not made for these parties,' she said, looking at the girls dancing on the floor. Most of them wore short clothes, had coloured hair and flaunted expensive accessories.

'Ms Counsellor, as you said, we go to places for ourselves, not to fit in with other people. Happiness is not in the place or the people, it is within us. So let's dance!

Nobody is going to judge you here.' Madhav looked into her eyes and Radhika felt her insides unclench.

'I seriously doubt the kind of therapist you are if you're so anxious about a silly club. Smile please,' he said, putting her at ease.

They walked towards the bar. 'I will have a tequila shot. What about you?' Madhav looked at Radhika. She seemed to be at a total loss. She gawked at the different brands of alcohol on the shelves.

'Umm, well, I don't drink,' she mumbled.

'What? Tell me you are lying,' he said.

'I mean, I used to, but it's been a long time.'

'Let's just let loose tonight, Radhika,' he said and asked the bartender for two tequila shots.

They looked at the people dancing and grinding to the latest hits. 'It all seems so pretentious sometimes. These expensive clothes, the make-up . . . just to project a certain image,' she said, in a deprecating tone.

'Not tonight, please. We should discuss these things during our next meditation session.' She snickered as the bartender put down two shots in front of them.

'Bottoms up?' he asked. She nodded as he counted down from three and they knocked back the shots. He laughed as she rubbed her chest at the burning sensation.

'One more?' he asked and to his surprise she said yes. They had three shots, screwing up their faces at the strong aftertaste.

The DJ changed the music to old-school tunes and 'Love Hangover' by Diana Ross came on.

'We have to dance to this,' she said and turned towards the floor.

'Are you the same Radhika? Or is this the alcohol talking?'

'Oh just come on!'

'Oh no! Dancing isn't my thing,' he said.

'Let's let loose tonight, Madhav!' She winked at him and took off her heels.

'But I look dumb while dancing,' he whined.

'Just follow my lead,' she said. He couldn't say no after hearing the excitement in her voice, so he followed her to the dance floor.

Radhika swayed to the music, her hair billowing as she gracefully moved her body.

'Just copy me.' Madhav tried to do so, but he was too mesmerized by her. He couldn't believe that this was the Radhika he knew. Her moves were extraordinary.

'I didn't know you danced so well,' he shouted in her ear. She laughed and held his arm as they both got into the groove.

'You've got it!' she said, catching her breath. As they moved in sync, their bodies listening to each other's rhythm and nothing else, Madhav could feel himself falling for her all over again.

The beat quickened, and she pulled him closer. They were only inches apart. This was the closest they had ever been and he could feel her sweet breath on his face. The DJ played a few romantic songs for the couples next. It was close to midnight. Madhav felt like holding Radhika in his arms and lifting her in the air as a sudden surge of exuberance boosted his spirits. She put her hands on his shoulder while he held her around the waist. They forgot everything around them and as they drew closer, he leaned in to kiss her and her vision blurred. She stepped back for a moment before coming even closer than before. Her nose touched his scruffy beard and then found his lips as she closed her eyes and stood on her toes. Madhav closed his eyes too and moved his mouth closer to hers. Their lips pressed together for a brief moment and they melted into one another.

In the next instant, Radhika pulled back and opened her eyes, looking at Madhav. Her heart was pounding at the intimacy.

'I am sorry,' she whispered softly and walked away quickly, leaving him flabbergasted. He ran after her as she wiped her lips and put her shoes back on.

'Radhika!' he called after her but she didn't look back. He ran faster and grabbed her hand.

'What happened, Radhika? Why did you run off like that?' he asked, even though he had his suspicions about her odd behaviour.

'This isn't right, Madhav,' she said, still unwilling to look at him.

'What do you mean?' he asked.

'We can't do this . . . I mean, I can't do this. These clubs, this lifestyle . . . it's just not me. I can't be with you.' Tears caressed her eyelashes as Madhav held her hands tightly.

'Don't say that, Radhika. You've taught me how beautiful life can be. Why can't you accept that fact for yourself too?'

'Because I can't love anyone! Forget it, you won't understand.' She looked frustrated and pushed his hand away. She walked towards the car park and Madhav followed her quietly. The sound of her heels and their laboured breathing were the only things that broke the silence. They stopped near his car, shivering in the cold night. She wrapped her silk stole around herself and looked at the sky.

'I love you, Radhika,' Madhav said.

'No, Madhav. This is not love. You have no idea how often this happens. People think they're in love with their therapists all the time because they feel grateful to them, so don't mistake it for love.'

'But I genuinely love you, Radhika. Why won't you just believe me?' he beseeched.

She finally looked at him and said, 'I can't and won't believe you. I am not made for love. I am older than you, Madhav, and I have experienced things in life that you are still exploring.'

'How does that matter?' he asked.

'Everything matters.'

Madhav groaned and looked up at the moonlit sky. Radhika wrapped her hands around herself, her breath condensing in the increasingly cold night. He wanted to hold her and share the warmth.

'Please drop me back home,' she said finally. 'And please find a new therapist for yourself.'

Madhav didn't say a word. Radhika wanted to cry, but controlled her tears. They reached her home in silence and, as she got out of the car, he rolled down his window and said, 'Happy New Year, Radhika!'

She stopped and turned back. Their eyes met, expressing the love they unequivocally shared, asking a million questions but answering none.

She fought back the lump in her throat and replied, 'Happy New Year, Madhav! I am sorry.' She walked to her apartment and he gazed at her silhouette until she disappeared up the stairs. 'I love you,' he said softly and drove back home. He parked the car in a forested area a few hundred metres away from his house. He scowled with frustration at himself in the rear-view mirror. He decided to sleep in the car as he didn't want to face anyone that night.

10

Madhav woke up in a bed. He rubbed his eyes and looked around, but his vision remained blurry. He could see the faintest ray of moonlight penetrating the room through a small window. He got off the bed and his feet kicked an empty glass bottle aside. The bottle rolled on the floor and hit the wall, making a clanking noise.

He looked around, trying to focus his vision. Radhika was sleeping next to him, curled up in a warm blanket. He walked out of the room, confused. He remembered that they had had an argument and he had dropped her home, eventually deciding to sleep in his car. Then how was he at her house?

It certainly was Radhika's apartment, a beautifully decorated white space with Kutch art on the walls. He walked into the foyer, shirtless. He unlatched the main door which opened on to a wide staircase. As he descended the stairs, he could tell it was very late at night, almost close to dawn. But the dark, serene night had no answers for him.

He stood in the middle of the road, half-conscious. He walked barefoot towards a wooded area. The shadows of the trees outlined his path. He saw the silhouette of a small boy on a wheelchair amidst the huge pine trees. The boy raised his hand and waved, asking Madhav to come near. Madhav walked in a daze towards the boy. As he went closer, the shadow disappeared and suddenly reappeared right behind him. He was startled and he staggered. He couldn't see the boy's face but he knew it was someone very close to him. The shadowy figure morphed into three separate figures and they played around merrily, pretending to pluck fruits from the trees. Madhav smiled and knelt on the ground and felt as if his childhood memories were coming to life on this dark night. The shadow in the wheelchair was now in the middle of the road, calling out to him.

'Madhav, please save me!' He heard the familiar voice of the young boy. He closed his eyes and, smiling, went near the shadow.

'Madhav!' Someone shouted from behind him but he paid no heed to it. He felt his soul crawling out of his body and a strange force compelled his body to do its bidding. As a loud honk broke his trance-like dream, he saw that he was lying on the roadside, against the grassy sidewalk. A truck roared past him. He opened his eyes wider and looked up.

'Madhav, please!' Radhika stood in tears, tugging at his hands.

'Radhika,' he murmured. He was covered in sweat as his body shivered. 'Where am I?'

'Madhav, what are you doing? You were having a fit in the middle of the road,' she cried.

He held Radhika as she sobbed. 'Please come back home.' Pulling him to his feet, she took him upstairs and made him sit on the bed. She calmed herself down and tried to figure out the best way to approach the situation, her therapist's training kicking in.

'Where am I?' he asked.

'We're in my apartment,' she said, placing her palm on his cheek.

'What are we doing here?' He looked around. The window was now closed. Radhika was wearing a short red nightdress while Madhav realized he was half-naked, wearing only his jeans. His shivering worsened.

'Last night you came back here,' she said. He nodded, pretending to remember.

'What happened to you?' she asked, handing him a bottle of water.

'I don't know. I thought someone was calling me. I went down and saw young children playing.' He had a sip of water. 'And then you came.'

'And before that?'

'I felt like two people in one body. It was like my soul was crawling out and I was losing my senses.' He took a deep breath. Radhika went closer, trying to decipher what he was saying.

'I don't remember how I got here,' he finally confessed.

Radhika could discern a few things but was still extremely confused. 'It's okay, Madhav.' She kissed him lightly and he drew back, shocked at her gesture. He remembered she had rejected his advances last night.

'But you left me alone last night,' he muttered.

'Madhav, you came back here sometime during the night,' she said, rubbing his back.

'And what happened after that?' he asked uneasily, deeply perturbed at his loss of memory.

'Nothing. You just asked me if you could read a book and sleep here tonight.'

'Read a book?' he asked. His confusion deepened but he desperately wanted to know if Radhika had accepted their relationship.

'Did you agree to be with me?' he murmured, sipping the water.

She smiled at him and pecked his cheek to calm his roving thoughts.

'I will tell you everything, Madhav, but I want you to relax right now. We can meet in the evening. And yes, Happy New Year, silly boy,' she said sweetly, ruffling his hair.

Convinced that he was all right, Radhika asked Madhav to head home. He drove back, puzzling over the forgotten events of the night, but smiling at the fact that he and Radhika were finally together.

~

Radhika wasn't certain what was happening to her but more than that, she was extremely worried about Madhav's hallucinations, which had almost killed him.

She was unsure about the underlying trauma, but it was clearly harrowing for him. After spending hours going over every detail of the case, she finally decided to discuss it with her mentor, Dr Geeta Lodwal. She called her up and fixed an appointment with her.

Dr Geeta Lodwal was a renowned psychiatrist who ran an institute called the Cosmos Institute of Mental Health and Behavioural Sciences. She was a kind woman with a highly keen intellect, whom Radhika respected immensely. She had had plenty of experience with rare cases such as Madhav's and Radhika was sure that she would be able to shed some light on this case.

Dr Lodwal greeted her warmly as Radhika walked in.

'How's your practice coming along?' Dr Lodwal asked.

'Work is good, but this one case is proving to be quite difficult,' Radhika said, cracking her knuckles.

Dr Lodwal went through Madhav's file, pausing to ask Radhika a few pointed questions.

'You wrote post-traumatic stress disorder as your initial diagnosis but the symptoms don't quite match,' Dr Lodwal said.

'Yes, that is what confused me, doctor. His recurring claim about a different personality inhabiting his mind and body, the memory lapses and out-of-body episodes all point to something quite different from PTSD. Last night, he forgot he came back to my house and spent time with me. He was a different person altogether. I tried to talk to him but he insisted on reading a book and slept.

He then had a very dangerous episode. But he cannot recall most of it, which is quite troubling.'

'Well, you are right. It's too early for us to definitively say he has PTSD or even some other disorder. Do you have any idea about the childhood trauma he might have suffered?' she asked.

'No, doctor. I tried to evoke memories of an incident in his past that I've been suspicious about for a while now, but he never talks about it.'

'These symptoms are not enough for us to conclude anything and repressed memory can be a symptom of many disorders. Patients with borderline personality disorders or bipolar disorders also suffer from it. They forget conversations and sometimes wouldn't even remember where they were or what happened to them a while ago. I suggest that you carry on with cognitive behavioural therapy and also create situations that lead him to open up,' the doctor advised.

Radhika nodded. Madhav didn't remember that while she had turned him down the previous night, they did get intimate in certain other ways. But she hadn't completely accepted their relationship yet.

'Most importantly, you need to contact his family so that they can give you some idea about his past because it is unlikely that he will open up of his own accord,' Dr Lodwal added as Radhika was still lost in her own thoughts. 'Do you like him?' she asked.

'No, doctor! I mean . . . it's not like my relationship with other patients. There's something special about him. I'm growing emotionally close to him and I'm not sure

I want to.' Radhika struggled to verbalize her feelings without divulging too much.

'I have known you for a long time, Radhika. You usually discuss all your cases in a very professional manner with me, but this time I can see worry in your eyes and concern in your voice. I know you're struggling with your own issues but you can't let that affect this particular relationship if you want him to open up to you.

'There are no rules or laws when you follow the path of love. But there is a difference between a therapist and a lover. If you want to be his lover, then you have to learn to be open and vulnerable. I'm saying this as your friend. As your professional guide and mentor, I would like to remind you that this is unethical. If you want to remain his therapist, you need to put aside your feelings for him. You can't have a dual relationship.'

'I understand, doctor. The truth is I really like him but at the same time I am scared, especially after what happened in London with Christian.' Radhika finally articulated her real fear.

'I'm aware of what you are going through but if you genuinely like him and care about his life, then trust your love and go ahead without hesitation. If it's becoming personal, then treat it that way. You're not just his therapist any more, so there's no point pretending otherwise. Don't tell yourself again and again that his love is not true or what you feel is just momentary. I know you are a great therapist, but apart from that, you are also a beautiful human being and you have all the right to love and to be loved.'

Radhika realized that she hadn't been able to fully commit to analysing Madhav's case because she was torn between her personal and professional selves. It was a tough call for her. She couldn't think practically when it came to him. She decided to take the plunge and talk to him as openly as possible and to let her feelings and instinct, instead of cold logic, dictate her relationship with him.

'I discontinue my practice as a therapist officially, doctor. I cannot do justice to my profession as I am not allowed to love and heal at the same time. And I will choose to love,' she said.

'I appreciate it, Radhika. Make sure you take each step carefully. I trust you.'

She left Dr Lodwal's office and texted Madhav.

'*Could you come to my place in the evening with flowers and pastries, like you did the last time?*'

Madhav was lying in bed, staring at the ceiling fan and thinking about the previous night. He was fed up with his memory lapses. His phone beeped. Radhika's message made him smile.

He typed, '*Yes, but the ones I brought last time are still with Suresh.*'

She laughed aloud and replied, '*I think I deserve fresh flowers and a chocolate truffle cake.*'

Madhav reached Radhika's place late in the evening. He was in the front hallway when he saw her sitting at her study table. It was a dark, cosy space; dim yellow fairy lights adorned the wall. He walked towards her study and knocked on the door.

'Is your main door usually open or did I just get lucky?' he asked.

'You are an exception,' she said. 'You can see the house as it is now and as it will be forever.'

She had beautifully painted her walls and decorated it with embossed mud art. Each corner of the house reflected her aesthetic sensibility. She was painting a portrait of a naked woman with a wild, happy expression on her face. The woman had a red sari draped around her head instead of her body and her arms were wide open.

'What is this?' Madhav asked.

'Freedom, of a sort,' she said. 'She's ready to fall in love.'

'Looks interesting,' he said and sat on a beanbag. 'Are you going to paint the entire time I am here?' he asked as he put on some light music.

'Nope!' she said and stood up. 'We are going to dance.'

Madhav smiled and asked her about the reason for her sudden romantic behaviour.

'I want us to pick up where we left off.' She drew the curtains and switched off the main lights. A small lamp and the fairy lights softly illuminated the room. Madhav offered her the flowers. She elegantly took the bouquet and placed it in an empty vase. She then began to lightly sway to the music, almost as though she were dancing purely for herself. Madhav tried to decipher her mood. It occurred to him that her painting might just be a self-portrait. Radhika held his hand and put on an old Bollywood number '*Ek ajnabee haseena se yun mulaqat ho gayi*'.

'This song pretty much sums up my situation,' he whispered in her ear as she twirled on his finger held high above their heads. Madhav smiled at her and began singing along with the song. They danced for a while until he no longer felt restless.

'What happened last night?' he asked calmly, and Radhika paused,

'Before I tell you anything, I want to share something with you.' She rested her palm against his cheek. He instinctively knew that she was going to take a leap of faith and finally tell him why she had been so reticent.

'Okay, of course, Radhika,' he said as they sat by an open window. Radhika's pink curtains billowed in the chilly breeze. She lit a small lamp and began her story.

'It was seven years ago. I lived in London with my family. I was pursuing clinical social work and, as a part of the course, the professor asked us to prepare a few case studies. We visited different hospitals to talk to patients. I was just twenty-two then. One day, I met a guy named Christian. He was admitted to the local government hospital because he suffered from severe anxiety attacks. I took up his case. He was a young man who worked as an event manager in central London. We began to meet and talk several times a week—he would share his problems with me and I would listen intently. I was told that therapists are not supposed to forge personal relationships with their patients until they are cured, but I failed to listen. Christian and I became good friends. We would go out for dinner regularly and talk for hours. I would open up to him as well, once in a while. During this time, he was diagnosed with bipolar disorder. He reacted in extremes; sometimes he was very happy and then extremely angry.

'My feelings for him deepened and then one day he called me home. I was young and naïve and thought he was going to ask me out. That night he told me he loved me and wanted to spend his life with me. I said yes, overjoyed to start this welcome chapter in my life. But later that night he told me that he was already married and that his wife and daughter lived in the Netherlands. He said he would leave them and marry me, but I couldn't bear that he had lied to me this whole time. I refused and he became angry. He tried to force himself on me but I resisted. Somehow I managed to escape and left London that very night. Later he emailed me saying that he never loved me and only needed a shoulder to cry on.

'I completed my research in India on special request. My parents have been asking me to come back to London but that incident has left a deep scar on me. I even thought of leaving this profession, but my mentor made me realize that therapists are human after all and thus, vulnerable too. I became a workaholic and did not get involved with anyone for years. I treated all my patients with utmost professionalism and even kept friends at arm's length because I was scared someone would take advantage of me again.

'That night, with you at the club, all those memories came flowing back and I reacted out of fear. I am sorry, Madhav. I am really sorry. I don't want to hurt you, but I don't want to suffer either.'

Madhav held Radhika by the shoulders and kissed her forehead. He was reminded of the way he had treated Meera. He felt bad and wanted to apologize for trying to force Radhika to open up earlier, but this was not the right time.

'You scared me! The way you began your story, I thought it was going to end in murder,' he joked, trying to make her smile. 'So you decided to not love any more because of one unstable man? I understand he hurt you badly, but you can't give up on love because of the way he treated you,' Madhav said.

Radhika nodded and he kissed her forehead again. She asked him hesitantly, 'Are you going to leave me?'

'Leave you? I want to live with you, Radhika! I don't want to just grow old with you, I want to live every single moment with you, no matter how trivial. I love the way you listen keenly to people. And I'm not saying this just because you listened to my problems. I love the way you care for each person around you. The way you talk and paint so freely, the way you dance so elegantly, the way you drive your scooter, the way you puncture tyres—I love everything about you!' he said.

Radhika laughed and planted a kiss on his cheek. 'I didn't want to keep any secrets from you, Madhav. I want to destroy all the barriers between us.'

Madhav evaded her gaze, feeling guilty because she had opened up to him while he was still afraid to do so, afraid that she might leave him if the truth was revealed.

He tried to change the topic. 'When exactly did you fall for me?'

She punched his arm playfully in response.

'No! You have to tell me!'

'I never fell for you. I rose with you,' she said. 'Thank you, Madhav. You make me feel so special.'

'Wow! You sound like a poet,' he said.

'No, Madhav. You are the poet. Please start writing again,' she said.

Madhav stood up and changed the song to '*Afreen*'.

Radhika sang along with the female vocalist, '*Jaane kaise baandhe tu ne ankhiyon ke dor . . . Man mera khincha chala aaya teri ore . . . Nazron ne teri chua . . . Hone lagi main haseen . . .*'

Madhav joined in, '*Usne jaana ke taareef mumkin nahi . . . Afreen Afreen . . .*'

They melted into each other's arms. Then they walked silently towards the bedroom.

'You wanted to know what happened last night?' Radhika asked.

'I want to know if we're going to spend every night together,' Madhav said and hugged her, holding her tight against him, an embrace that made her feel safe and tingly at the same time. He kissed her. Her face flushed and her eyes shone. She dipped her fingers in some paint that was on the table and trailed them across his face.

He sprinkled a few drops on her bare arms and back as she removed her shirt.

'Am I finally going to see your tattoo tonight?'

Instead of answering, she reached for him, putting her small, warm hand on the back of his neck, lifting her lips to his. They kissed, at first lightly, then more urgently, his tongue in her mouth, her hips tilted against his, her breasts against his chest. Her body was sending her a message that was undeniable. She took Madhav's hand and placed it over her tattoo as he finally got a glimpse of it. It was a beautiful angel with wings spread across Radhika's shoulder blades. He moved closer and kissed the angel.

'You know, you're quite smart. Last night I told you to sleep on my couch but you promised to behave if I let you sleep on my bed.' She dragged her nails down his arm.

'You are just irresistible. I can't help it,' he said and pulled her on to the bed.

She switched off the lights and they kissed again. Her tongue fluttered against his and his hands were buried deep in her soft hair. It was as if time had ceased to uphold its laws, carrying them right back to when they'd met for the first time.

He pulled her against him, feeling as if he'd never get close enough to her. If only he could fold her inside him. He'd keep her warm and safe, always.

She nibbled his chin, his ear and, running her fingers down his face, asked. 'Why do you love me, Madhav?'

'You make me love myself,' he said. 'You brought me back. You have helped me become the person I used to be.'

He slid his hand between her legs, moving his fingers and thumb in a way that made her breath catch in her throat. He nuzzled her neck, nibbling and kissing his way up her earlobe. Radhika moaned over and over again. She gasped as he worked his way up her slick centre, losing herself in rediscovered pleasure.

Neither of them spoke, simply revelling in the feeling. Radhika had one hand on his shoulder, the other slowly stroked his back, from the nape of his neck to the base of his spine. She put her lips against his ear, whispering his name over and over again, like a chant, a song, a prayer.

When they finally came down from the high, she rolled into his arms and said, 'I love you! Thank you for coming into my life, but you should've come sooner!' With her hands balled into fists, she punched him lightly on the chest, like it was his fault they hadn't met all this while.

'I love you more,' he said. 'I feel like . . .'

'What?' she asked.

He remembered how she'd tried to elicit something more than just a 'fine' or 'happy' or 'tired' when she had asked him how he felt.

'I feel as if I'm complete. When I'm in your arms, it feels like I've come home,' he said and smiled. He'd been smiling so widely these past few hours that he was sure his face would ache in the morning.

'I love you. I will always love you, more and more every day,' he said.

11

Madhav sensed Radhika had got up when the bed creaked. He slowly came out of a deep slumber, feeling as though he'd gone to sleep only a few minutes earlier. But when he groggily opened his eyes, it was broad daylight and Radhika lay on her belly beside him, dressed for a jog. She cupped her face in her hands and beamed brightly.

'I'm sorry to wake you up, Madhav. I know you slept very late but I thought you'd want to know.'

He blinked, yawned and asked, 'Know what?'

'That your mother called and I spoke to her,' she said and dove beneath the blanket.

Madhav was up in a flash and yelled, 'What?'

'And she has invited us both over.'

'Look, it's the second of January, not the first of April.' He couldn't believe his ears.

'She said she's very happy to see you looking better these days and she wants to meet the person responsible for it.' Pride filled her eyes.

'What did you tell her? Did you tell her we slept together?' he asked.

'Madhav Mehra, I am not that stupid,' she replied. 'I told her there was a get-together at my place and that you and a couple of friends had stayed the night. I said I had answered the call as you were still asleep. Then she began asking about me, but it turns out she already knows a lot. I was a little embarrassed. She said I should come home with you.' Radhika didn't tell him everything that she had told his mother as she had a plan to enlist Mrs Mehra's help during this visit.

'My mother is becoming cool.' He pulled Radhika towards him and kissed her.

'Mr Sleazy, I have breakfast ready for you. Come!' She pulled him to his feet and took him to the small dining area. There was a large banyan tree painted on the wall behind the table.

'I wish I could wake up like this every morning,' he said. Radhika had set out toast, cereal and milk on the table. 'You said you'd made breakfast. Where is it?' He narrowed his eyes.

'What do you think this is? It's what I eat.' She picked up an apple and waved it in front of his face.

'So you will never make aloo ke paranthe?' He made a puppy-dog face.

'No, Mr Mehra. I also want you to give up your unhealthy lifestyle and become fit.' She ruffled his hair and combed her long fingers through it.

'Fit for what? Am I not able to . . .' He winked.

She tapped him on the head. 'Eat fast and get ready.'

Sated and energized from their meal, they made love. Madhav went back to sleep while Radhika left for a jog. They loved spending time with each other; her exuberance and his boyish innocence aligned perfectly.

~

Madhav stood in front of his house with his arm around Radhika's waist as he rang the doorbell. He assured her that his mother would definitely like her. As he bent to kiss her on the forehead, his mother opened the door. Radhika quickly drew away from him and hugged his mother, asking, 'How are you, Aunty?'

Madhav, his lips still puckered, came forward and hugged his mother too. She wasn't used to such warmth and care from him. 'I am fine, beta. How are you?' She was a little disconcerted by Radhika's hug as she was expecting her to touch her feet as per tradition. As progressive as she was, deep down Mrs Mehra still had a bit of the conservative left in her. She scanned Radhika's outfit—a blue kurta, tight white leggings and a shawl. She looked very pretty. Mrs Mehra finally smiled.

'Ma, if you're done with your inspection, can we come inside?' Madhav asked.

His relationship with his family was improving day by day. Radhika had helped him realize that relationships with family and friends were the roots that nourished a healthy person. She wanted him to connect with his family in order to disconnect from what was troubling him. She wanted him to blossom in love, to rise in love.

As they settled on the couch, Mrs Mehra asked the help to bring in drinks and snacks. She finally turned to Radhika and asked, 'So, are you a psycho?'

'Mom!' Madhav was flabbergasted. 'It's psychoanalyst, not psycho!' He gnashed his teeth in annoyance. Radhika couldn't help but laugh.

'What exactly do you do?' she inquired further.

'Radhika is a therapist,' he explained.

'Not any more,' she muttered to herself as Madhav gave her a wary look.

'I am talking to her, Madhav,' his mother replied and turned towards Radhika.

'What is your full name?' she asked.

'Radhika Kapoor,' he said.

'Madhav,' his mother said, 'did you notice your names?' Madhav and Radhika both looked baffled. 'Madhav is one of Lord Krishna's names and Radhika is Goddess Radha,' she said with a beaming smile. 'They were also five years apart in age.'

Radhika gave a little start. They had not told anyone about their relationship since they knew the age gap would raise eyebrows in their traditional society.

The maid brought samosas and biscuits and placed them on the table.

Madhav was afraid his mother would start talking about his childhood. He ate one biscuit after another, trying to assuage his nerves.

Every time she came close to broaching the topic, Madhav changed the subject, but the women seemed adamant on talking about it.

'Radhika, I want to show you some of our family albums.' His mother asked Radhika to join her in the other room. It was a spacious room, mostly unfurnished except for two chairs and a table full of trophies. The walls were adorned with medals, certificates and framed photographs.

'This room belonged to Madhav when he was a child, before he shifted upstairs,' his mother said wistfully. The room brought back memories of a happy and joyful Madhav and she missed him terribly.

'Madhav won all these medals?' Radhika asked.

'Yes. Once he returned from Nainital, he worked very hard and excelled at everything he did.'

Madhav hadn't entered the room. He paced anxiously outside. He called out to Radhika a few times but she didn't respond as she had her own agenda.

'Nainital? Madhav was in Nainital?' Her curiosity was piqued.

'Yes, he studied at Nainital Hilltop School.' Madhav overheard his mother and finally stepped into the room to end the conversation before it went too far.

'Radhika, let's go upstairs. I need to show you something,' he said, panicking, but she ignored him and continued to look at a class photograph that hung on the wall. She went closer to the sepia-tinged picture to read what was written at the bottom. It said, 'Nainital Hilltop School—Batch of Class IX/Year 2000–01'.

Radhika tried looking for Madhav in the photograph but something else caught her attention—a boy in a wheelchair. He wore thick spectacles and had a vibrant smile. She looked for his name in the list below—Parth Aggarwal. Radhika felt a strange shudder go through her body. Her instinct told her that Madhav's present condition had something to do with this boy.

Mrs Mehra handed over an old album to Radhika. It documented Madhav's life, from infancy to his teenage years. Some of the photos were of him receiving awards for poetry competitions. She slowly flipped through the pages. The same class picture was a part of the album. She turned the page and what she saw made her knees go weak.

A photograph depicted the scene Madhav had painted in her art therapy session. Two boys on a hill, one in a wheelchair with the other's arm around his shoulder. But in this photograph, she could see the boys' faces. It was Madhav and Parth in their school uniforms, holding a trophy with cheerful smiles on their faces and not a care in the world. She stared at the picture, scrutinizing every inch of it and then looked at Madhav. She had found a hint but the larger riddle remained unsolved.

Madhav looked at her and then at the album. He saw the picture from a distance and came closer, staring at Radhika, terrified for a second, before snatching the album from her hands and yelling at them, 'What are you trying to do? What do you think will happen? Tell me! Tell me!'

His mother looked worried but Radhika was secretly pleased with this reaction since it indicated that his issues were, in fact, connected to his friend, Parth. Madhav ripped the photograph out of the album and yelled at his mother, accusing her of ruining his happiness. He began throwing the medals and trophies on the floor, screaming, 'These are not mine! They were never mine!'

Radhika asked Mrs Mehra to stay calm as Madhav ran upstairs with the album. His mother, stunned by the sudden outburst, shakily sat down. Radhika brought her a glass of water.

'I knew this would happen,' Mrs Mehra said.

'Who is Parth, Aunty? What happened between him and Madhav?' Radhika asked, sensing that she was finally close to unravelling the mystery.

Mrs Mehra closed the door and sat next to Radhika. She looked out of the window, at the trees in the garden, and said, softly, 'He died.'

Radhika was aghast. Her worst fear had come true.

Mrs Mehra continued, 'Madhav joined Nainital Hilltop School when he was ten years old. He was very happy there. We would visit him often and he would come home for his winter holidays.

'He met Parth on the very first day of school and soon, they became best friends. Parth was, unfortunately, a paraplegic. When Madhav came home for his holidays, he would tell us about Parth—how they were like brothers. We have met him a few times. He was such a nice boy. Despite his disability, he would top every exam. He was a genius. But one day, we received the news that Parth had fallen off a hilltop behind their school. It was reported as an accident; no one else was present when he fell. People said students would go there to smoke or drink and, because of that, there were many rumours surrounding the incident. We were so shocked to hear this and were worried about how Madhav would take this. The school authorities informed us that Madhav had been deeply traumatized by the incident and wasn't eating or sleeping properly. They asked us to visit him and when we got there, we were shocked to see him. He spent hours sitting on Parth's wheelchair with a glazed look in his eyes, not responding to anyone. We were scared and so we decided to bring him back to Delhi.

'Even after he reluctantly returned, he would sit quietly in his room. He did not make friends in high school or even in college. His father was busy with his business and his sister was studying abroad, so they weren't able to help him with what he was going through. He stopped writing poetry and began studying, relentlessly, day and night. He topped his senior secondary examinations and then his university.

'But he stopped interacting with us. He would abruptly get angry at the littlest of things. He would talk to his reflection in the mirror. He would do or say things that he would later forget. The rest of us began fighting with each other since we didn't know how to cope with his behaviour. He would lock himself in his room and study the entire day. He often complained of severe headaches and on some days he would say that he couldn't feel his legs, that his vision was blurry. We were seriously worried that he was gravely ill.

'We took him to various doctors but he misbehaved with all of them. However, we secretly medicated him, which helped suppress some of his violent impulses and mood swings. Some doctors said he was bipolar, others said he was depressed, but no one could successfully diagnose him. We believed all of them out of desperation. While we were happy that Madhav was doing so well academically, we were concerned about his erratic behaviour.

'Since you've come into his life, I have seen him get better; he has started interacting with us and is smiling more than ever. I have this feeling that only you can help my son, Radhika. So many therapists have talked to him and prescribed medicines. But only something beyond that can bring the real Madhav back and that is your love. Please don't give up on him. Help bring our son back.'

Tears welled up in Mrs Mehra's eyes as she shared what was in her heart. Even though she didn't know exactly what had happened to Madhav after Parth's death, her maternal instinct told her something connected to the incident was haunting him. Radhika held her hand and said, 'Aunty, I promise I will help your son.'

Mrs Mehra smiled and kissed Radhika's palm. 'He loves you so much. I have seen it in his eyes,' she said.

Radhika knew there was more to the story than what she had just heard and it was up to her to help Madhav confront his demons.

She was now sure that it wasn't merely a behavioural disorder that caused Madhav's strange episodes, it was something he had kept buried for years. Something has been festering inside him and had a dark, malicious hold over him because he has been repressing it instead of dealing with it. She knew she had to recreate certain circumstances to elicit an honest confession from him, to make him realize the truth of his condition.

Radhika bid Mrs Mehra goodbye and left, knowing that Madhav had locked himself in his room. She didn't go upstairs to meet him because she knew he wouldn't respond and sensed he needed some time alone.

12

It was a chilly January morning in Delhi and the excitement of the New Year had just about died down. Radhika sat on the couch in her balcony as the 7 a.m. fog swirled around her. She sipped coffee and read the newspaper, her glasses perched on her nose, wrapped in a woollen shawl. It had been a day since the incident at his house and Madhav had not called or messaged her. Radhika wanted to give him enough time to dwell on things so she decided not to call him either. She decided to work out a plan, but what happened next threw a wrench in the works.

She was browsing through the business page of the newspaper when her doorbell rang. Too lazy to get up immediately, she waited for a minute, but the bell didn't ring again. Putting the newspaper aside, she shuffled towards the door. Her bare feet slipped on the polished marble floor and she fell on her side with a thud. 'Oh damn,' she cried. She got up, her back aching a little, and walked to the door. There was no movement on the other side. She opened the door but saw no one. As she was about to close it, she noticed a small white envelope lying on her doormat. Her back hurt as she bent down to pick it up. She looked around once again, quite perplexed by the appearance of the mysterious envelope. She ran back to her room and peeked through the window that looked out on to the street. She saw a shadowy figure, wearing a black hoodie that obscured its face. The physique and gait seemed quite familiar to her.

Her phone rang as the man disappeared into the fog. It was an unknown number. She didn't answer and instead sat on the couch and looked at the envelope. Her mind was still reeling from the story Madhav's mom had told her.

Radhika sipped her coffee, which had become cold by then. The envelope had a fine layer of dust on it. It was sealed with a yellowing piece of sticky tape. She wondered how old it was. She turned it over and noticed a logo on the front that looked like the emblem of a school. Her address was written with a scratchy blue ballpoint pen in a familiar handwriting. She finally tore it open. The letter itself wasn't handwritten but typed out. But before she could start reading it, her phone rang. It was the unknown number again. Her heart pounding, Radhika finally answered it.

'Hello,' she said, with trepidation.

'Ma'am, I am calling from Vodafone. We want to share the details of our post-paid plans. We have some new offers for you,' a rushed voice blurted out. Radhika was annoyed but calmly replied, 'I am busy. Please call me some other time.'

The morning sun peeked lazily through the fog. She switched off her phone and focused on the letter.

Hello Radhika,

I hope you are doing well. You must be drinking your morning coffee and reading the newspaper right now. I have known you for a while now, you see. And now that you know me too, I thought I must write to you.

We have met several times before, though you may not be aware of it. I have seen you and Madhav laugh, talk and love. You've made him experience love in a way he never has before, except perhaps once, a long time ago. I know that you love him very much and want him to heal. I wish you luck because I want to be free. I don't want to live with him any more. He has captured me, not only in his brain, but also in his soul, his heart, his consciousness. He hasn't let go of me. He has been striving to be the person I always wanted to be. He has been dying each day so that he can live the way I always wanted to live. His dreams have been forgotten, his life is in a shambles.

Oh! I forgot to tell you my name, though I'm sure you must have guessed it by now.

I am Parth Aggarwal.

I am not dead yet. I live inside Madhav. I am festering inside him and with each passing day, he

is becoming more and more helpless to stop me. But
your presence and light has helped diminish my power
over him. I don't know how much longer you'll be
able to hold me at bay, but for both your sakes, I hope
you can help him win this battle.

Love and power to you,
Parth

Her heart pounded louder with every sentence she read.
She had been treating patients for six years but this
went beyond anything she had ever come across. It was
intensified by the fact that it was happening to someone
she loved. This completely changed her intended course
of plan for Madhav.

She read the letter a few more times to try and wrap
her head around what was happening. Who was the man
who had left it at her door? Was it Madhav? Her brain
worked furiously and then something struck her.

She threw her shawl aside and ran out. She looked up
and found a CCTV camera right above the main gate of
the society. She then went to the security booth, looking
for the guard.

'Bhaiyya, for how long do you keep the CCTV
recordings?' she asked.

The guard looked clueless. 'Madamji, I don't know. I
need to ask my boss,' he said.

'Shit!' Radhika muttered as the guard went back to
his booth and dialled a number on his phone. After a
quick conversation, he returned and said, 'Madamji, we

keep the recording for a day, but you will have to wait till my boss comes. He knows how to access the footage.'

Radhika thanked him and went back home to call Dr Lodwal.

Once she had arranged a meeting with her mentor, she returned to the security booth, where she was grateful to find the senior guard waiting for her.

'Bhaiyya, I want the video footage from that camera,' she said to him, pointing at the CCTV camera at the main gate.

The guard took her inside the booth. On his computer, he opened a folder where the recording of the day was stored. He played the video and they saw a view of the empty street at 6 a.m.

'Please forward it,' said Radhika. 'I want to see from 7 a.m. onwards.' The man forwarded the video. They saw the newspaper delivery boy, the milkman and a few people out jogging. Radhika's eyes were glued to the main gate. She was looking for a man in a black hoodie. They saw a figure approach the gate at 7.10 a.m. Radhika still couldn't see his face clearly.

'Pause it, please,' she said and then zoomed in on the man's face. Even though the image was blurry, she knew who it was.

'Madhav,' she uttered as the guard looked at her. She took a picture of the image on her phone—of Madhav walking down the street in a black hoodie, a white envelope in his hand. He wore a pair of thick black spectacles that she'd never seen before. She clutched the letter tightly in her hand. It was Madhav who had left the letter on her doormat. In a bizarre way, she had elicited the sort of reaction she wanted from him and she now had a clear idea of what might be tormenting him. But she still couldn't understand the crux of the problem. She needed to discuss it further with Dr Lodwal and figure out a way to finish this once and for all.

13

Radhika was walking into the institute with her case file in hand to meet Dr Lodwal when she received a call from Madhav's mother.

'Hello, Aunty! Is everything okay?' she asked.

'Beta, Madhav has been behaving very strangely since yesterday. He locked himself up and wouldn't come out of his room. Then, without any warning, he left home early this morning. I have been calling him since seven but there's been no answer. I am really scared,' his mother said.

'What was he wearing?' Radhika asked, just to be certain.

'He was wearing his usual outfit. A black hoodie and jeans,' she replied. 'He couldn't have gone to office like that, so I don't know where he might be.'

'I will try to find him, Aunty. Please don't worry. He will be all right,' Radhika comforted Mrs Mehra and went in to meet Dr Lodwal. She was worried about what

Madhav might do in his current state, but first she needed to review the morning's events with Dr Lodwal.

On the other side of town, Madhav was nonchalantly walking towards his office, not bothered that his clothes were strictly against the office dress code. He felt he was beyond any sort of rules that day.

As Radhika entered Dr Lodwal's clinic, Madhav entered his office.

'It's been quite a morning,' Radhika said to her mentor. She showed her the letter and explained what had happened, starting with what Madhav's mother had told her and ending with the CCTV tape.

Dr Lodwal, astonished by what she had just heard, put on her thick spectacles and began reading the letter.

In Madhav's office, there was another kind of storm brewing. He walked into Mr Rao's cabin, clearing his throat impertinently to get his manager's attention.

Mr Rao looked up and scanned Madhav's attire. Madhav took off his hood.

'What is this? Don't you know—' But before his manager could start on his tirade, Madhav laughed humourlessly and said, 'I know! I know everything. I know that I should be wearing a shirt and a pair of trousers with socks, polished shoes, a tie and your company's bloody dog tag!'

'Do you even know what you're saying? Are you drunk? We hired you barely a month ago!' Outraged, Vinesh Rao threw his hands in the air. Madhav mocked him and laughed.

'You know, Mr Rao, employees don't leave companies, they leave managers like you. Ninety per cent of your staff hates you. You make this place an absolute hell and you don't give a damn about the people who are forced to work for you in this hellhole. And they don't have a choice because they need the job and you exploit them. Did you know that the main topic of conversation at the after-hours drinking sessions is what a crappy boss you are!' Madhav taunted.

'I will blacklist you!' Rao said as people walked by his cabin and whispers rippled across the floor.

Madhav scoffed at him. 'I resign!'

Vinesh Rao was banking on Madhav backing off and apologizing. Instead, Madhav threw his resignation letter on the desk and showed his boss the middle finger. Before walking out of the office, he said, 'Stop treating your employees like slaves. Make sure you are remembered for something good in life.' A couple of people flashed him covert smiles of approval as he left.

Madhav had locked himself in his room to write these letters which clearly revealed that there were two sides to his personality. He wrote his resignation letter, which stressed the importance of his dreams. The other letter he wrote as Parth, realizing the need to be annihilated from Madhav's life. He also wrote a third letter to Meera, apologizing for his behaviour.

Dr Lodwal put down the letter and looked at Radhika. 'This is a case of DID,' she said.

'Dissociative identity disorder,' Radhika muttered. She had suspected the same.

'It's not PTSD as you'd earlier thought. His recent actions make that very clear,' the doctor replied. 'Your attempt to glean information about his past by telling him your issues and meeting his mother seems to have worked.'

'Yes. It did work, doctor. But now I'm scared. I have never handled such a case before and this happens to be a person I love—it makes me feel so helpless. Is it really DID?'

'This is what it looks like, Radhika.'

'It means that the night he came and asked for the book, it was not him?'

'Yes, Radhika. His alternate personality rarely comes out in public or maybe it's yet to become a part of him completely. This is exceptional and terrifying at the same time.'

'What should I do now?'

'I know you do not share a therapeutic relationship with Madhav any more, but the only way to complete recovery is to expel Parth's personality, leaving behind one integrated self. Madhav's alternate personality expressed the desire to be expelled so Madhav's true identity can take over completely. Only you can convince him to let go of Parth. Just tell him that he doesn't need Parth in his life. You can't do it as a therapist, but you can surely do it as someone who cares for him deeply.'

A tear rolled down Radhika's cheek.

'Radhika, you have come so far and I am proud to see how patiently you have dealt with such a personal case. If you can try just for a little while longer, I think you can facilitate the final breakthrough in this case. I think only you can make this happen because no one else has made this much progress with Madhav before. You're closer to resolving this than you think.'

'What should I do next? I'm contemplating going to the site of the trauma and rekindling those memories to begin the final healing process,' she said.

'Yes, Radhika. We're still unclear why Parth's death caused this disorder. It's obvious that a large part of Madhav's life has been dictated by what he considered to be Parth's desires—the medals, the achievements, the corporate job, they're all at odds with Madhav's real desires. Only you can resolve this dissonance because he doesn't seem to respond to anyone else.'

'But how do I do this, doctor?' Radhika was desperate.

'First, you should go to Nainital.'

'With Madhav?'

'No, go alone. Go to his school, find out what happened all those years ago. Then try to get a clear idea of what happened before asking Madhav to join you. You can then confront him,' the doctor said, confidently.

Radhika knew that it was going to be incredibly difficult but she believed that this was the only way forward and she trusted their love enough to know that they would survive the tough times ahead.

Dr Lodwal added, 'The additional identity is usually created by the patient in order to survive some sort of psychological trauma and feel protected. Even if this personality is created during childhood, it persists even after the trauma has subsided. In this case, it's affecting

Madhav and those around him quite drastically. We have to isolate the cause and treat it. How do you plan to do that?'

'We will have to place him in a similar situation, but only after he tells me what really happened on that hill,' she replied.

Radhika decided to leave the city the next day. She wanted to tell Madhav's mother but she decided it would only worry her unnecessarily.

'Stay in touch, Radhika. I have faith in you. You are not only a good student but a great human being too, and I know when it comes to helping someone you love, your will knows no match.' Her mentor's words reassured her.

Radhika left the institute and booked a ticket to Nainital for the next morning. She then checked her phone and found a surprise lying in store for her.

'*I have resigned. I listened to my heart. Thank you!*' Madhav had texted.

She smiled for the first time that day, glad he was making decisions for himself. But she was acutely aware of the possibility that his altered personality wouldn't accept this decision easily. This might create more friction and confusion in Madhav's mind. Radhika could see that their love was helping ward off Parth's influence but she knew she had to find a permanent end to this.

She reached home and packed her bags, determined to get to the bottom of his closeted past.

14

Radhika woke up earlier than usual. She got out of bed and realized she had fallen asleep in her jeans and jacket. She freshened up and checked her backpack once again, before putting on her shoes and leaving the house, thermos in hand. She would need the extra caffeine.

She boarded the bus to Nainital in the misty darkness. The sun had not yet shown its face. Her thoughts wandered back to when she had first met Madhav and she smiled at the recollection of his naïve and unrestrained displays of affection, his charming boyishness and his silly antics. She had always been fatalistic and was sure now more than ever that the universe had brought them together so they could help one another overcome their respective pasts. Only then could they truly be together. She dozed off in the light of dawn.

A cool breeze caressed her face as she awoke. She stared at the Kumaon foothills through her window.

The mighty Himalayas loomed in the distance. It was awe-inspiring, but Radhika was unaffected by nature's grandeur as she was preoccupied with the thought of what was to come. As the bus trundled through the meandering roads and hairpin bends, the smell of pine trees soothed her agitated mind. The temperature began to drop as she reached Haldwani, a small town in the foothills, and she could feel a strong chill descending upon her.

Dwelling upon the events that brought her to this point, Radhika realized the extent of her love for Madhav. Despite his condition and her own emotional problems, she felt they shared something pure that transcended their circumstances. She saw glimpses of this purity shining through the dark patches in their tumultuous relationship. It was worth fighting any battle to save what they had.

The bus reached the Nainital bus depot a few hours later. Radhika googled the exact location of Nainital Hilltop School and booked a cottage nearby. She bought plums from a roadside vendor and ate them as she walked through the town, observing life in the quaint hill station. The Christmas and New Year crowd had just left. The streets were deserted except for a few stragglers wandering about. Despite the snowfall, there was bright sunshine. Radhika sat on a bench under the naked sky, silently and slowly letting her thoughts melt into nothingness.

She stood up and hit the road again, eventually reaching a narrow, rocky trail snaking up a mountain.

It was a steep trail, and she walked so fast that she could hear her heart pounding in her ears. She smiled, feeling alive.

She finally took a taxi and reached Nainital Hilltop School, perched high up on a mountain. She could see the tranquil pear-shaped Naini Lake from atop the hill. She looked up at the huge school building, adjacent to a church. A narrow lane ran between the church and the school, leading to a hilltop. Was that the same hill? Radhika got out of the taxi and walked towards a big gate that guarded the school. The wide path that led to the main building was bordered by lush green trees. There was a crest on the main gate, same as the one on the envelope that contained Madhav's letter.

A security guard came and asked Radhika, 'Madam, may I help you?'

'I have come to meet the principal,' she said. The guard was an old man. It occurred to her that he might have been around for a while so she decided to question him as well.

As she filled in her details on a register at the gate, she asked the guard, 'How long have you been working here?'

'It's been twenty years, madam. I live in a nearby village,' he said.

He seemed forthcoming so she decided to explicitly ask him what she wanted to know. 'Do you remember an accident that occurred at the hilltop behind the campus? It involved a boy in a wheelchair,' she asked, reading his expressions carefully.

The guard mulled over her question for a few seconds and said, 'Yes, yes, I remember. But that's a very old incident. Since then that route has been out of bounds to everyone.' He pointed to a narrow lane between the school building and the church.

'What else do you remember?'

'Not much. However, I do remember that some local villagers had reported finding the wheelchair dangling from a tree and the boy at the bottom of the hill. The students were not allowed to go there. At that time there were no cameras in the school,' he said and smiled at her, ruefully.

'That's it? Anything else?' she asked, slightly disappointed.

'No, madam. I am just a guard. I do as I am told. I just remember that it was difficult to recover the body. Then the school was on lockdown for a few days.'

Radhika handed the register back to him and thanked him. She then walked towards the main building.

The school looked more like an ancient castle or an old British manor. The grey buildings were topped with red domes. There were children in winter uniforms playing in the basketball court. She tried picturing a young Madhav and Parth standing on the sidelines. A few kids sat in the park in front of the main building. The campus was peaceful and quiet. Radhika looked at her watch—it was 11 a.m., probably lunchtime.

She asked a cute little girl who was sipping water from her Pokemon bottle, 'Where is the reception, dear?'

The girl smiled at her and pointed to a small door. Radhika pulled her cheeks playfully and walked towards the reception, looking at the children and reminiscing about her childhood. She stepped inside a huge room, full of trophies, and walked up to a desk where there sat a pretty woman.

'Hi! I would like to meet the principal,' Radhika said to the receptionist.

The girl looked up at her with a vibrant smile. 'May I know the purpose of your visit?' she asked.

'My name is Radhika Kapoor and I am from Delhi. I wish to speak to the principal about conducting workshops for children,' Radhika lied to the girl, knowing that her real reason would sound very odd.

'Okay, madam. Let me just check with his secretary.' After a short conversation on the phone, she said, 'Father Nelson has gone to the church. Please wait for a few minutes.'

Radhika walked around the room, looking at the photographs and trophies. She wandered into a small alcove where she found pictures of students who had won scholar medals in the past. She slowly scanned the wall for the batch of 2000–01. She stared at the picture of a young boy with a bright smile and thick spectacles— Parth Aggarwal. There were no pictures of Madhav. Radhika connected the dots: Madhav had taken on Parth's scholarly ambition after leaving school.

'Father Nelson is here, madam,' said the receptionist, bringing Radhika to the present. She turned around to see an old man walking towards her.

Radhika introduced herself to him. The man smiled at her warmly and asked, 'How may I help you?'

'Father, I need to discuss something personal,' she said, hesitantly, as he guided her to his office.

'Have a seat, dear,' he said, briefly touching the Bible as he sat behind his desk. A holy cross was affixed on the wall behind him. The shelf on the right was full of books, plaques and certificates.

'Father, my name is Radhika Kapoor and I'm from Delhi. I wanted to talk to you about Parth Aggarwal and the accident that happened in 2001,' she said firmly.

'The thing is, my dear, I came here only in 2008. Every four years the principal changes. At the time it was Father George, I think. All I know is that the poor boy fell off the hilltop and died.'

He stood up and wiped the fog off the window and pointed towards a hill. 'That was the hill. It is strictly out of bounds to students now.'

Radhika looked at the now-familiar hilltop from Madhav's painting and the photograph. It was a beautiful, grassy hilltop, with wild flowers swaying in the breeze.

'Would you happen to know anyone who could tell me more about the incident?' she asked.

'Sister Stella was here during that time. She would remember the case better than anyone else,' he said. Then, looking straight at her, he asked, 'Is everything all right, dear?'

Radhika nodded and said, 'Yes, Father. Everything is fine. Where can I meet Sister Stella?'

'Sister Stella is old and almost bed-ridden, Radhika. I could give you her address, though. She lives nearby,' he said.

He handed her a slip of paper with an address on it. 'I don't know what you're looking for, but I hope the Almighty gives you the strength and love to deal with it.' Father Nelson smiled at Radhika as she got up to leave. A strange energy filled her being and compelled her to keep going until she accomplished what she had set out to do.

Sister Stella lived in Sangudi Village. On the way to her house, Radhika stood by Naini Lake and gazed at the mountains.

She should've been tired, but she wasn't. She checked her phone but there weren't any texts from Madhav.

She called his mother to ask if she knew where he was. 'Hello Aunty!'

'Hello Radhika,' she said, softly.

'How's Madhav?' she asked.

'He seems pretty stable. He told us that he quit his job. Mostly remains shut up in his room.'

Radhika was surprised. Madhav hadn't tried to contact her. She told his mother not to worry and disconnected the call.

She slowly walked down the dusty street, humming old Hindi songs. The sky seemed to have been set aflame and a cold wind whistled through the trees. Realizing that it was getting late, Radhika walked fast towards Sangudi Village. She had tea and toast on the way and asked the owner of the teashop for directions.

Radhika finally reached Sister Stella's home, an old cottage situated on the outskirts of the town. She walked through a small garden and arrived at the main door on which was inscribed a quote:

Jesus turned, and seeing her he said, 'Take heart, daughter; your faith has made you well.'

The words resonated deep within Radhika's soul and she felt buoyant and confident that she wouldn't fail Madhav. She rang the doorbell.

A young boy opened the door. The house looked rather shabby but spacious. 'I want to meet Sister Stella,' she said. The boy ran back into the house yelling, 'Momma, someone has come to see Aunty Stella!'

A middle-aged lady appeared from the dark recesses of the house, with a cake box in her hand. She looked inquiringly at Radhika.

'Hello, my name is Radhika Kapoor. Father Nelson sent me here. I want to speak to Sister Stella,' she said.

'Come in,' said the woman.

Radhika sat on a slightly moth-eaten sofa as the woman called out to Sister Stella.

A very old woman, with wrinkled skin and liver spots, hobbled towards Radhika. She must be in her eighties, Radhika thought.

'Yes, my dear,' she said, making her way on to an old rocking chair. She couldn't speak very coherently, so Radhika moved closer to hear her properly.

'Hello Sister, I am sorry for bothering you. My name is Radhika and I have come from Delhi. I wanted to speak to you about something that happened eleven years ago at Hilltop School,' Radhika said, deciding that plunging right in was the best way to begin.

'What happened eleven years ago?'

'A boy called Parth Aggarwal died,' she said. Sister Stella looked at her stunned.

'Why are you asking me about that day?'

'I am Madhav Mehra's friend. I think that incident might be the source of his present illness,' Radhika explained.

'Poor child! I remember he was in shock,' she said.

Suddenly, Radhika's phone rang—it was Madhav. She disconnected the call, but he kept trying, so she put her phone on silent mode.

'Could you please tell me what exactly happened?' Radhika asked.

Thankfully, Sister Stella turned out to be quite garrulous for her age.

'It was winter, if I remember correctly. Madhav and Parth had been joined at the hip since their first day at school, but they were quite different—Parth excelled in academics while Madhav was known for his poetry. They were a trio—there was a girl too—and the three of them were together all the time. Of course, being a faculty, I don't know much but I remember the two boys were like brothers. On the day of the incident, we couldn't find Madhav for a very long time.'

Sister Stella shook her head and continued, 'Something had happened prior to the fall and Madhav was almost expelled from school, but before any official action could be taken, we received the news about Parth's demise. As there was no witness or any evidence of foul play, it was treated as an accident. But I was somehow never entirely convinced. After Parth's death, Madhav began behaving very erratically and cultivated strange habits. We thought it would be best if his family was around him during that time, so his parents took him back. I don't remember much about that girl, but she also left shortly.'

'Who was the girl? Why don't you think it was an accident?'

'I don't remember her name. As for the incident, I think there might have been more to the story. Parth was a very cautious boy and he didn't seem like the sort to drink and lose control at all. But who knows? Maybe it really was a freak accident. That's what we all ultimately accepted anyway,' Sister Stella said, her eyes moistening.

Radhika had heard almost all of this from Madhav's mother but there had been no mention of a girl. There was only one person who could help her make sense of this increasingly confounding story. She bid goodbye to Sister Stella and thanked her for everything, kissing her wrinkled palms.

Radhika walked back to her cottage. The trees stood like silent observers of the mountains, rivers and clouds. Or perhaps they looked like mourners at an invisible funeral. The dark sky was dotted with silver stars.

Radhika realized it was time to call Madhav and put the last pieces of the puzzle in place. Only he could complete this story.

She lit a lamp in her cottage and browsed through her old notebook. She came across a piece she had written a long time ago.

There is a place at the end of the sky, where the earth kisses the moon, and that's where, someday, I will bring you back.

When you have walked enough, and hurt enough, there I will help you find your peace.

You'll realize it's everywhere and nowhere, and always within you, if only you take the leap and fly to the edge of the horizon. In that somewhere, I will bring you back.

She smiled as these words of love gave her courage and called Madhav. His phone rang for an agonizingly long time.

'Radhika! Where are you?' Madhav asked.

'Madhav,' she replied, trying to brace herself.

'I asked you something. Where are you?'

'I am in Nainital,' she said. There was a deafening silence for a few seconds.

'I am in Nainital, Madhav,' she repeated.

'Why? Why did you . . . you didn't tell me,' he whispered, sounding fearful.

'Did you tell me that you were going to resign?' she countered.

'But you always wanted me to resign.'

'And now, I also want you to tell me the truth,' she said, her resolve enveloping each word and vibrating through to him. 'You will have to come here if you love me, Madhav. Otherwise you will never see me again.'

Madhav was reeling. He couldn't say no, he couldn't bear to lose her. But his mouth couldn't form any words.

'We will never be together if you don't meet me in Nainital,' she threatened him, hating giving him an ultimatum, but knowing it was the only way.

'Okay, Radhika. I'll come to Nainital.'

15

Madhav left for Nainital despite his mother's protests. Worried about her son, Mrs Mehra called up Radhika who assured her that this trip to Nainital was crucial.

Meanwhile, Radhika went back to his school and asked the authorities to let her go to the hilltop. Father Nelson gave her permission only after she told him about her suspicions and what she planned to do.

Radhika walked down the narrow pathway that led to the hilltop. She felt the frosty blades of grass crunch under her feet as she walked. She breathed in the faint traces of the happy memories and the horrible tragedy that hung heavy in the air. They were carved into the barks of the trees against which the two boys had sat many times, dreaming about their future.

It took Madhav seven hours to drive up to the hill station. He hadn't returned to Nainital since he'd left as a boy and the memories came rushing back to him. He felt as though he was going to confront his younger self.

Radhika sat on the hilltop for a while, thinking about what she was about to do, as she faced the wind, feeling its icy touch.

The school was closed for the weekend, so it was extremely quiet, almost uncomfortably so.

Her phone rang. It was Madhav.

'Radhika, I am here,' he said and she could hear the uneasiness in his voice.

Madhav looked at the gate leading to the hill and almost broke down. It had been eleven long years since he had last walked that path. Memories flashed in front of his eyes. He could see himself running in his school uniform, following Parth in his wheelchair to their favourite place.

He instinctively knew where to find Radhika. He had been preparing himself to face the place that haunted his dreams, but the familiar acidic feeling rose in his throat and he knew the other voice inside him would try to resist her love and help.

His heart skipped a beat as he walked up the hill. His breath caught in his throat and he almost turned back several times, but the thought of losing Radhika prevented him from succumbing to his fears. He could see her standing on the hilltop. Her silhouette against the familiar backdrop only intensified his fear and he breathed deeply, trying to stop the barrage of emotions from overpowering him.

Radhika knew what she needed to do. Madhav had to reveal the truth he had been hiding all his life, one that had completely taken over his identity and made his existence a lie.

'Radhika,' he said, shakily, as he walked up to her.

She turned to look at him. She looked angelic in a black sweater and a long skirt. Silver bangles adorned her wrists while a small bindi decorated her forehead. Her brown hair tumbled gloriously down her shoulders and her eyes shone with her love for him.

'Why are you doing this to me?' Madhav asked. The freezing wind blew this way and that, as capricious as his thoughts.

'What are you doing to yourself?' she asked, her voice deep with concern for him.

'What do you want to know?' he yelled. His nerves were so taut that he felt as though his head was going to explode.

'I want you to tell me the truth, that's all. I want you to let go of the burden you've been carrying with you all these years. I want you to live, Madhav! Live as yourself, not some gruesome, twisted version of someone else.' Radhika spoke as earnestly as she could, not wanting to aggravate him further.

'What do you want to know?' he asked, his voice ringing through the valley below. 'What do you want to know?' The veins on his neck were now visibly throbbing.

'I know everything, Madhav. I just want to hear you say it,' she said, trying to calm him down.

Madhav went down on his knees, groaning as though in pain, his face buried in his hands. Radhika held his shoulders, caressing him, her warmth easing his pain a bit.

'I killed him,' he said abruptly, his words piercing through the air. Radhika's hands fell from his shoulders and she crumpled on to the grass next to him as her knees gave way in shock.

'Did you know this? Did you? Of course you did not!' She numbly watched his face contort in pain.

'You killed Parth?' she asked, hardly recognizing the words that left her mouth. She had suspected that Madhav was a witness to Parth's death, but never once had it occurred to her that he might have caused it.

'Yes, I killed him. I killed Parth.' Madhav broke down. Radhika didn't have the strength to hold him. She draped her shawl across his shoulders and waited for him to speak. 'That is why I have kept him alive inside me,' he said. 'It just happened, Radhika. I didn't mean to. Any of it . . .'

'What exactly happened, Madhav? I want to know.' She held his hand and sat next to him. The skies had turned a soft greyish purple and the wind had ceased its howling. Even the birds had returned to their nests, so it was calm when Madhav began to speak.

16

1996
Hilltop School, Nainital

Sixteen years ago, shortly after my tenth birthday, my parents got fed up with my troublesome, lazy ways and decided to send me off to boarding school. I wondered if I would fit in at my new school. I was scared to leave my parents and go. But I had to; I had no say in the matter.

It was my first day at Hilltop. It was a posh school with the kids of politicians and businessmen throwing their weight around. I missed my parents terribly and felt alienated by the moneyed lot.

My life always seems to take an unexpected turn as soon as I start predicting it. My first English lesson was in the lower sixth common room—a sunlit classroom overlooking the lush gardens and rolling hills. There were thirty-one students, nineteen of them girls. One of them was Shriya.

She was one of those pretty, doe-eyed hill girls for whom city boys would invariably pine. I was besotted with her. She had light greenish-blue eyes, a straight, sharp nose and cheeks fair enough to turn red in the chilly winters.

The geeky-looking boy with thick black spectacles I happened to be sitting next to was Parth. He turned to me after the lesson and said, 'Hi, can we be friends?' He was the first person to talk to me in that school. I noticed he was in a wheelchair. Though I was initially hesitant to befriend a differently-abled child like him, I realized how inconsiderate it is to undermine people like him. We shook hands and he smiled. It was one of the most beautiful things I'd ever seen.

After class, we spoke for hours. He told me his father had a transferable job and hence they had lived in many parts of the country. Since it became difficult for him to keep changing schools, his parents had decided to pack him off to boarding school. I told him my father was rich but had no time to look after us and discipline my sister and me, so he'd sent me here and my sister to the States.

We had an extremely strict schedule to adhere to in those days. The house sisters woke us up every morning at 7 a.m. by knocking on the door and yelling, 'Good morning, children!'

We were not allowed to go to the mess in our pyjamas, so we showered and got ready for school before breakfast. The girls ate their breakfast in a separate mess. We were served baked goods, fresh fruit salad, muesli, yoghurt and flavoured milk for breakfast. We had a food comment box where we could leave suggestions as well as a recipe of the month competition. The winning dish was cooked for everyone. Parth would always ask for chhole bhature, which never got selected. We had to attend PT before classes, which made our mornings even busier. Lunch was usually served outside the boarding house and we'd sit on the grassy Boarders' Lawn to eat. We often saw our 'big sisters' around that time. They were like our matrons and regularly checked on us to see if we were doing all right. Ours was Sister Stella.

Parth and I spent our days there together. There was a helper to take him to the bathroom, but I tried to be there for him at all times. So, in all, we studied together, played together and, unfortunately, fell in love at the same time too. That was when everything changed.

I'd always been fairly good at English but had never really been too passionate about it because I didn't like the way it was taught in school. We slogged through our prescribed texts, memorized the key quotations and rehearsed answers to the essay questions for the exams. It was mind-numbingly methodical and pedestrian. That is when I discovered the joy of writing, frustrated with this dogmatic way of teaching and learning. Writing poetry actually made me feel alive and I delved into this world without hesitation. While I found my passion in poetry writing, Parth's ambition was to pursue management studies.

By the time we were in class nine, Parth and I had developed a special bond. We would go everywhere together—the small hill, Tiffin Top, Naini Lake and the local market on Mall Road. He started smoking around that time. I asked him not to make a habit of it, but he claimed that it helped him concentrate and study. From talking about our favourite cartoons to rating the girls who passed by, we did all the typical teenage stuff. We didn't have Internet access in school, so our friends were all the entertainment we had.

Next year, I got an A in English and flunked all the other subjects. During the subsequent PTA meeting, I was told to buck up or I'd be expelled. I would've been in a lot of trouble had Parth not helped me get through the final exams.

'I don't want to study this crap, Parth. I want to write, that is my dream,' I said to him one evening on the hill, as he lit a cigarette.

'Just live life your way, Madhav. You know I'll always stand by you.'

That year, Parth won the Student of the Year award and a photographer was called to the school for a shoot. We had our batch photo taken that day. Parth and I persuaded the photographer to come with us to the hilltop and had him take a photograph of us with Parth's trophy.

I still remember the pride and love I felt for him at that moment, at our special place, convinced that he would be there for me forever.

We entered the dreaded class ten in 2001, and had to make our first career choices. Shriya had grown into a gorgeous girl by then. Students from other sections would come to the Boarders' Lawn to catch a glimpse of her during the break.

One day, after school hours, afternoon tea was being served in the courtyard and everyone was relaxing with their friends. Unless we had art club meetings to rush off to, we just basked in the sunshine.

My literary prowess helped keep me in the school and also made me popular as I started writing for the school magazine.

That day, I was writing something while Parth was cramming history notes. I recited a few lines that I had written about our friendship.

No matter how far or near,
You are always there
Forever in my heart
You will be for years and years . . .

He smiled at me as the sun shone on his face. Before I could complete the poem, I saw Shriya walking towards us. The most beautiful girl in the school came up to me and said, 'I love your poems, Madhav.'

Parth and I both looked at her and then at each other. Shriya had never spoken to me before, apart from monosyllabic exchanges such as 'Thanks' or 'Hi'. And now, here she was, actually complimenting me! Everyone sought her out but she was rather picky about her friends. I'd been wanting to talk to her for years, as had Parth, I was sure.

'Thank you,' I said to her. Parth elbowed me. 'Will you ever say anything more than that?' she teased me with her beautiful smile. It was mesmerizing.

'Actually he's shy around girls,' Parth said and giggled. They laughed at me and high-fived each other.

'I am not shy around girls, okay? In fact, I like talking to them. By the way, which of my poems did you like?' I asked, putting on a show of self-confidence.

'I liked the one . . . umm . . . the one .. .' she said, squinting in embarrassment.

'Did you even read my poems?' I asked as Parth snorted. I looked sharply at him and he dove back into his notebook, trying to control his sniggering.

We all burst out laughing. That was when it all began. Shriya had lied about reading my poems but it didn't matter because she liked me. We grew closer and often spent time alone, which made Parth jealous. She would ask me to take her to the hilltop and we'd sit there for hours while I recited my poems.

At the same time, Parth helped Shriya with her studies. They would sit for hours in the classroom, slogging over maps and graphs. He helped her score better marks in all the subjects and over time, we became a tight-knit trio.

We always chose the last row in class so that all three of us could sit together. Shriya and I always defended Parth against the occasional ignorant bully who would try to make fun of his disability and so no one messed with him. Though we were envious of his intellect at times, we knew that our journeys were different.

Shriya told us about her dream to pursue modelling. She had won almost every local beauty contest, but her parents were against her going to Mumbai to chase her passion. Parth advised her to focus on her studies and trust that the rest would eventually fall in place.

It was 2001. I vividly remember one night when Shriya and I were sitting on the hilltop. No one was allowed off campus after 9 p.m. but a few students knew about a secret path that led there. The seniors would go there to smoke up and juniors like us would go there to nurture our budding romances.

That was the first time Shriya held my hand. I was dizzy with that intoxicating feeling of first love and wrote a few words for her.

A love so precious, a love so new
A love that comes from me to you . . .

We ran back to our dorms that night, our faces aglow with love. Parth asked me why I was smiling so much but I didn't tell him. I thought he already knew that Shriya and I liked each other.

Shriya had become even more gorgeous by then. Boys from the senior sections came to our class to try to get a glimpse of her while most of the girls in our school were jealous of her.

She still wanted to be a model while I aspired to be a professional writer. Our unconventional passions connected us and we talked about the hurdles we would face in pursuing these dreams. Parth, on the other hand, was a scholar. His research papers were already being published in international magazines and he was nationally recognized for his exceptional intellect.

After the winter holidays in October, Parth went to Delhi for a minor knee operation. Shriya and I were left alone and we spent a lot of time together, talking and writing. She would pick random topics or objects and ask me to write poems about them. On one such winter evening, we came to this very same hill to watch the sunset. We'd started doing this daily, bunking our evening classes. She held my arm and I remember becoming even more attracted to her.

'Madhav, your words make me so happy. They . . . you . . . make me feel alive,' she said. The orange skyline indicated the imminent onset of darkness. Grey clouds covered the sun and proceeded to welcome the stars. Slowly, evening turned into night and we kept moving closer to each other. We hadn't confessed our love to each other yet but she took the plunge.

'I love you,' she said. I looked at her, my heart banging against my ribcage. She tucked a lock of hair behind her ear and looked up at the faint stars.

'You're so beautiful, Shriya, just like this twilight.' I kissed her ear gently. She was startled by my gesture. I went closer and kissed her cheek. She turned her face to reciprocate. It was our first kiss.

'I have always loved you,' I said and cradled her face. She came closer and we kissed for what felt like an eternity, until darkness blanketed us. We confessed our love repeatedly to one another.

'Parth will be so happy to hear about us.' I was excited to tell him about this new turn in my life.

'I think we should tell him as soon as he comes back,' Shriya said. We thought no one would be happier for us. But Parth wasn't expected to return for a few weeks and, during that period, our burgeoning romance blossomed until I was certain that this was indeed true love.

~

As the exams drew closer, Shriya got to know that she was nominated for Miss Teen Himachal. She ran up to me excitedly in the courtyard after lunch.

'Madhav, my dreams are finally coming true. You're my lucky charm.' She pulled my cheek and planted a kiss, after making sure no one was around.

'What about the exams, Shriya?' I asked.

'Don't worry. I will manage,' she said.

We saw Parth coming towards us in his wheelchair, a huge, joyful smile on his face. We ran towards him.

'I missed you, brother,' I bent down and hugged him. Shriya ruffled his hair. He looked up and held her arm. 'I missed both of you,' he said and I thought I noticed something in Shriya's eyes as Parth looked at her. He did not let go of her hand for a long time.

'Parth, I have news for you.' Shriya flopped on to the grass.

Before she could tell him, Sister Stella came up to us and said, 'You should let your friend rest for some time.'

'Sure, Sister,' Shriya said. Sister Stella told Parth to come with her to the dormitory.

'See you in the dorm, buddy!' Parth said to me, giving me a brief wave.

'I think we should tell him after the exams. Let's focus on studies now,' I said. Shriya nodded and gave me a quick kiss before Sister Stella turned to look at us.

Parth's operation had been successful. He started practising to walk with his crutches every day, slowly becoming more confident. Since he spent most of his time exercising and studying, we didn't get to spend much time with him.

The half-yearly exams ended and Shriya left for the pageant's state selection round. Parth and I went to wish her good luck at the main gate. That was the last time the three of us were together, basking in the joy of true friendship.

~

During the study holidays in November, Kumaon hills shuddered in the peak of winter. The days were short and the nights were relentlessly cold. There was a high footfall of tourists during this time as always. Away from the hustle, we huddled within the walls of our school, trying to keep ourselves warm.

The day Shriya was supposed to return, Parth and I thought of killing the time by playing basketball. He sat on his wheelchair at the free-throw line and I at the three-point line.

'Come on, boy!' I said as Parth hit the ball against the backboard. But his gaze was fixed on Shriya who was walking towards us. Her aura was truly magnetic.

'Hey, champs! I got selected. I am leaving for the nationals tomorrow. My father finally gave me permission.'

'All the best, Shriya.' Parth went closer to her and gave her a good-luck hug. 'You are so beautiful that no one will even come close to you. I think, like Madhav, I am also learning how to impress a girl with words,' he joked and stood up from his wheelchair holding his crutches.

'Thank you, Parth,' she said. She didn't hug him back, instead, she walked over to me and clutched my hand. 'I think you can beat him at anything you try, except for when it comes to impressing girls with words. He is the best at that.' She giggled a little.

'Congratulations, love,' I whispered in her ear. Parth looked at us intensely.

'Parth, we wanted to tell you something,' said Shriya. For some reason, I felt it wasn't the right time to tell him. Perhaps it was the strange expression on his face. I signalled Shriya to stop but she wasn't looking at me.

'Parth, I know you will be very happy to hear this. Madhav and I are finally in a relationship,' she said, with a beatific smile on her face. My heart skipped a beat. I could sense a strange fury in Parth's eyes. His crutches slipped from his grip.

'It's okay,' he said and bent down to pick them up, pushing away my attempt to help. 'Go ahead, Shriya.'

'That's it.' Shriya was slightly puzzled by Parth's reaction.

He then laughed loudly. We both smiled at each other in relief. But Parth wouldn't stop laughing. He sat back on his wheelchair and turned it in the other direction, still laughing. Shriya looked at me, slightly worried.

'I can't believe this,' he said, turning to us abruptly. His eyes were wet and I couldn't tell if they were tears of laughter.

'Are you okay?' I asked.

He rolled towards us, stopping inches away from me and looked deep into my eyes. His dark eyes held something I'd never seen before, sending chills down my spine. But he suddenly hugged me and said, 'I still can't believe this.'

His hug had no real warmth, seeming almost perfunctory. I could feel the uneasiness in his body language too. He was like my brother and I couldn't understand why he wasn't truly happy for me.

'But you have to believe it, Parth, because we're very much together!' Shriya came forward and held my arm. Parth stared at our tightly clutched hands with a fake smile plastered on his face.

'That's great! I am feeling quite tired. I should go back,' he said.

'Do you want me to walk with you to the hostel?' I asked. He refused and left the ground alone.

'What's wrong with him?' I asked Shriya.

'I don't know, Madhav, and I don't think I want to know. Maybe he's just tired today,' Shriya said, dubiously.

Then, shooting me a mischievous smile, she clutched my hand and dragged me into the gymnasium.

'What I do know is that I'm mad about my poet,' she said cheekily and started kissing me.

It was the end of the day and most of the students had gone back to their dormitories, so we were completely alone. There was absolute silence and we could hear our voices echo. Shriya had always been bold and liked to take risks that excited her. She pulled me further into the gym.

'Where are we going?' I asked her. She stopped and kissed me again. 'Just follow me,' she said. Behind the gym supplies was a door to a room that was empty except for a few rolled mats and a wall of mirrors.

'I have never seen this room before. How did you find this out?'

'We used this room to practise our ramp walk a couple of months ago. It mostly remains unused,' she whispered, locking the door. It was too dark for us to see each other's faces.

'Why are we here?' I asked, unable to comprehend her intent, even when she removed her blazer.

'I want to be yours before I leave for Mumbai,' she said, wrapping her hands around my neck. She threw her blazer in a corner and let her hair down. We were only sixteen and I was rather innocent. I had no idea what was going through her mind. Apparently, she had thought that we would get married once she became a model and I a famous writer. But the most I had thought about our future was her leaving for Mumbai in a few weeks.

She loosened her tie and unbuttoned her shirt, doing the same for me. I had never gone this far with anyone and, in a rush of adrenalin, I starting kissing her like I never had before. In the boys' hostel, we would talk and fantasize about making love to girls, but I had never thought that it would actually happen so soon. For some reason, thoughts about Parth and his reaction to our news kept flashing through my head.

Lost in thought, I didn't realize that we were almost naked. I reached for Shriya's breasts, unsure what to do with it but still enthusiastic. 'Do you know how to do it?' she asked, as we lay on a yoga mat. 'I'm not sure,' I confessed.

She grabbed my engorged penis and I moaned, whispering, 'This feels so good.' I tried to feel between her legs, wanting to touch her too. We both groaned blissfully. She put my fingers in her mouth and sucked on them.

'Put it inside me,' she said. I couldn't believe how confident she was, considering we were only sixteen. We had read magazines and books on sex in the science lab but only had a vague, clinical idea about it.

'Are you sure?' I asked, my hormones going wild. We were sweating on the severely cold evening.

Before we could've gone any further, a loud crash interrupted us. It sounded like a metal rod falling to the floor. The sound echoed and we realized someone was in the gym.

'Shit,' she muttered. 'Wait here,' I said as I put on my pants. I peeked through the keyhole and buttoned up my shirt. The sound of the wheels was easily discernible and as it became louder, I saw that it was Parth. Was he following us? I gestured Shriya to be silent. Parth came forward and tried to open the door.

'Who is it?' Shriya whispered as she put on her underwear. Parth left the gym after several attempts to open the door. I sighed and walked back to Shriya. She kissed my palm. We were just about to leave the room when we heard footsteps outside the room. I ran back to look through the keyhole.

What I saw made my balls shrivel up. Brother Stephen and two other faculty members followed Parth. 'Oh fuck!' I muttered. I finished dressing at the speed of light and asked Shriya to do the same. We started panicking.

'Open the door,' said the sports teacher. He was six feet tall and always carried a whistle with him.

'What now?' I whispered. We stared at each other, terrified, while they kept knocking.

Shriya opened the door. Parth, Brother Stephen and the two other teachers stood at the entrance.

'Madhav? Shriya?' Parth was wide-eyed, pretending to be shocked.

We were taken to the principal's office where Sister Sophia was also present.

'Sister . . . We were just . . .' Shriya mumbled. Our guilty expressions said enough. I saw Parth's eyes glint maliciously for a moment though his face was contorted in fake astonishment.

It was 8 p.m. and the whole campus was silent. The ticking of the grandfather clock was the only audible sound in the room as Father George sat in front of us, reading the daily hostel report. Behind us were Sister Sophia and the sports teacher. They asked Parth to go back to his dorm. He left quietly, shooting me an inscrutable look.

'Shriya Mathur. Hometown: Shimla; father: renowned businessman; nominated for Miss Teen HP.' Father George looked at her, his glasses sliding down his nose. Shriya looked down at her folded hands. Our clandestine moments rushed through my head but anger at Parth's betrayal overtook my shame.

'Madhav Mehra. Hometown: Delhi; father: banker; nominated for nothing.' He didn't even look at me. My heart was thumping loudly.

'According to this report, you were both caught in a restricted area, engaging in uncouth activities,' he said, his voice and eyes incredibly stern.

'This was not expected from you, Miss Shriya. We will not permit you to participate in the contest if you are found guilty,' said Father George. Shriya began to tremble and started sobbing.

'Father, please,' she begged.

'Explain what happened.'

She looked at me. She was stuttering incoherently and I had no idea what she was going to say. All I felt was pure rage towards Parth.

'Miss Shriya, I am asking you one last time. If you do not tell me the truth, I will take strict action against you both.' Father George banged on the table. He was a peaceful man, but could be merciless in such situations. Shriya looked at me again and fought a lump in her throat. She was quivering.

'Father ... Madhav ... Madhav took me to the yoga room. I didn't even know about the place. He said it would be dark and that nobody would find us there. Then he asked me to ... I'm too ashamed to say any more.'

A part of me died that moment, too horrified to feel anger or shock. I stood still for a couple of minutes as she broke down. All of it hit me in one go and it became almost too much to bear. What Parth did was one thing, but what Shriya did just ripped me apart. I was genuinely falling in love with her. I was intent on protecting her in this situation, but she took advantage of my love and lied to save herself. She looked at me, tears flowing from her eyes, every part of her being beseeching me to support her false accusation. I knew she was only doing this so she could still take part in the competition. She didn't want to lose her only chance, but I couldn't believe that she was ready to throw me to the dogs for a measly beauty pageant.

I stood staring blankly at the Bible on Father George's table. Everyone's eyes were on me. I realized I had nothing to lose, whereas Shriya had something to fight for. I felt a sense of nothingness taking over me and sighed, looking at Shriya one last time.

'Madhav? Is this true?' Father George asked.

I nodded in agreement. I just nodded. I could not say a word. I had lost my love and my best friend. I had never felt weaker. I had been deceived by the two people I had chosen to love.

'Do you want to say anything, Madhav? Or shall we end this discussion right here?'

I shook my head. There was nothing else to say. I decided I would never speak to Shriya again but I did want to ask Parth to justify his action.

Father George signed my termination letter and warned me to stay away from Shriya. He said he would call my parents after the final exams to make my termination official and that I was thrown out of the literature club, effective immediately. Shriya left the room weeping. But I somehow felt Parth's betrayal more intensely than I did hers.

Sitting outside the dorm, I wrote a poem that night, gazing up at the inky sky. That was the last real poem I wrote. The ones I wrote in college were just to look cool.

I gave you all I had
I tried to make it last
But now all we have
Are the memories from the past.

I went back to the dorm at midnight. Everyone was asleep. Parth's bed was next to mine. Every night I would arrange his things and his wheelchair so he wouldn't fall while getting into it in the morning. But that night he had done it himself. He didn't need me any more, I realized with a stabbing pain in my gut.

Exhausted, I jumped into bed but couldn't fall asleep for a very long time.

The next day was when I saw Parth for the last time. I never thought that it would end like this. I woke up and got dressed, feeling an odd pain in my body. I hadn't gone to sleep until dawn and even then, I had slept fitfully. Parth wasn't in his bed. We had a free day to either study by ourselves or attend extra classes. I walked out of the dorm and my eyes searched for Shriya and Parth.

I didn't see Shriya. I overheard her friends saying she had already left for the competition. I walked around the campus with a heavy heart looking for Parth.

'Have you seen Parth?' I asked a few batchmates when the evening classes ended. One of them told me he had seen him go towards the hill. 'What happened last night, Madhav?' asked Joffin, another classmate. The students knew that something had transpired between Madhav and Shriya.

'Nothing, Joffin. Excuse me, I need to see Parth,' I said and walked towards the hill through the playground.

I saw Parth sitting on the grass, his wheelchair next to him. He usually avoided taking his wheelchair to the hilltop when no one was around, just to be safe. I wondered how he had managed to find his way there without my help.

I stepped closer to him and asked, 'Why did you do this?'

Parth turned towards me. There was a lit cigarette in his hand. He was not wearing his spectacles that day and seemed like a completely different person to me. He blew a puff of smoke in my face.

'Why did *you* do this?' he repeated my question, harshly. The school premises had gone quiet by then. Dusk was slowly approaching.

'What do you mean, Parth? What did I do?' I had no idea why he was so spiteful.

'You did it deliberately!' he said.

'I still don't get it, Parth. Be clear for God's sake!'

'You knew I loved Shriya!' he shrieked. I didn't know my gentle friend was capable of such anger. He tossed the cigarette on the grass and his eyes blazed with rage.

I stared at him, dumbfounded. His words shook me to the core. I had no idea that Parth felt that way about Shriya. Although I had noticed a few awkward moments, like him deliberately holding her hand, asking her to spend time with him in the library or defending her in front of me, I'd always thought it was only because he was jealous that Shriya and I were close and that he also wanted to bond with her. How insanely naïve of me!

Parth struggled to get into his wheelchair. I stepped forward to help but he waved his hand in refusal.

'You knew everything. Yet, just to demean me, to rub my disability in my face, to show that all my academic achievements don't matter, to show off, you did this, Madhav!' He screamed so loud that the birds scattered from the tree.

'Are you out of your mind, Parth? I never knew this was what you thought of me and I definitely didn't know you loved Shriya. In fact, I thought you'd always known how we felt about each other! I thought you'd be happy to know that we were in a relationship.'

'Don't act smart, Madhav, because I am smarter than you and you know it. You knew I followed the two of you yesterday. I knew why you were going with her to the gym. I couldn't let you both make love. I knew that you liked her but I also knew that she liked me more than you. I was going to tell her how I felt once I was able to walk properly and get out of this damned wheelchair.' He punched the wheels as he rambled on like a madman.

'You cheated me!' I yelled, my eyes moistening.

'No, you cheated me! You're a cheater!' he replied.

'I can't believe this, Parth. We were like brothers. I was there whenever you needed me. I thought no one would better understand my feelings than you,' I said. I was devastated.

'Oh come on! I also helped you whenever you needed it. The only reason you are still in school is because I got you through. God may have given you the looks, but He gave me the brains. I know you did all this to prove that I am nothing compared to you. I am just a helpless, disabled idiot to you! You were always jealous of my grades, of my credentials, and you were afraid that Shriya would love me more than you. Do you think she likes your poems? Nobody likes your pathetic poetry! It means nothing. People love me and praise me; you were always jealous of that. You trapped Shriya!' He blurted out all the warped ideas and delusions that had been brewing in his mind for all these years.

I stood numb in disbelief. He had not just demeaned me but also obliterated the friendship we shared. Parth was rolling around in his wheelchair while spewing these poisonous words. I had never seen him in this state—it was frightening.

'Please, Parth, calm down and think about what you're saying,' I warned him. I wanted him to slow down as the gorge was very steep and in his frenzy he was headed in that direction.

'You should have minded your own business, Madhav. And what happened in the end? She dumped you, right? Because she never loved you, just like I don't love you. Nobody loves you.' I felt worse than I ever had. I even contemplated jumping from that hilltop. I didn't know anyone could carry such hatred in their heart.

'You know what, Parth? It's not your body that is disabled, it's your heart. You are a perverse person, incapable of friendship or love. I've always treated you like a brother, always supported you through difficult times, but never did I imagine that this was how you felt about me,' I said, calmer than before. Now all I wanted to do was hurt him emotionally, just as he had done.

'And even if Shriya had not been with me, she would never have gone out with you! You are a loser, a poor geek, with nothing but brains and which girl cares about that? She only used you to pass the exams.'

My words did something to Parth and he completely lost control. Parth had never been happy with his fate, which is why he wanted to become a scholar and get a high-profile corporate job. He wanted to prove to himself that he could get a girl like Shriya to love him.

He narrowed his eyes, screaming in murderous anger, and almost jumped from his chair to hit me. I grabbed his hands to stop him but he managed to hit my face. He slowly lost control of his wheelchair and it started rolling on its own. I tried to hold him but his flailing limbs prevented me from doing so.

'I love her!' he kept shouting as I tried to hold on to his wheelchair.

'She never loved you. She ditched you. She's mine!'

His attempts to punch me pushed him away from me. The wheelchair slipped on a boulder and tumbled downhill and Parth slid from it. His trousers were caught in the arm of the wheelchair and he dangled from the edge of the gorge, with the chair dragging him downwards.

'Parth!' I screamed, my blood freezing.

I ran to grab hold of his hand. There was a spine-chilling silence for a second.

'Madhav! Madhav! Please save me!' he said as tears ran down his face. His trousers were still caught in the wheelchair. My heart beat erratically as I looked around for help. Dusk had arrived and there was nobody around.

'Parth, just hold my hand tightly,' I said as our hands grew sweatier by the second.

'Madhav, please . . . save me . . . keep me alive. I want to live,' he whispered, his strength waning.

'Just hold on to me,' I said.

Slowly, we began losing our grip. I could feel his hand slipping away from mine. The chair swayed and pulled him down as the wind blew violently. It swivelled, thrusting him down towards the valley. I tried to hold on to him, but I couldn't and Parth fell into the chasm below.

Our fingers were intertwined for a few seconds before he fell. That was the last touch we shared. I saw him falling. I saw him suspended in the air, screaming for help. I can still hear that scream. Even after all these years. It is frozen inside me. That moment, I felt as though a part of me crawled out of my body and fell into the chasm with Parth. I lost something so close to me and, in that moment, I became what I had just lost.

It felt surreal. There's no other way to explain it. I thought I would wake up the next morning and Parth would laugh at me, maybe ask me to come play basketball. But he was gone. My heart stopped as I saw him falling. There was utter silence, the wind, the birds, the clouds, nothing moved. Everything seemed to momentarily die in that instant, including me. It was as if the entire world had ceased to be.

I looked around. It was freezing cold. I felt nothing. There was nothing left to live for. I tried to look for the slightest movement in the valley below, but saw nothing. What could I have done? Nothing! He was gone. I was young and weak. I couldn't think of doing anything, except running away. So that's what I did.

Had Parth died? I had no idea and the very thought of it made my insides churn. I ran as fast as I could. Was it right to run away? Maybe I should have called the guards, maybe he was still alive, maybe I would have saved him and explained what had happened, maybe he would still be here next to me on this hill, all these years later. I couldn't accept the fact that I had lost him. I thought I would see him in the dormitory, studying as usual. But he was not there. His bed was empty. His clothes, his books and his spectacles were all lying beside it.

I was so petrified. I didn't know what to do.

I picked up his spectacles and stared out of the window at the main gate of the campus, slowly digesting the fact that I had killed my best friend. I was flooded with regret, I was drowning in it. The regret of not saving him, of not being able to hold on to him, of not calling for help and of betraying him. It was so strong that it permanently changed something inside me.

As I went out of the boarding house, I heard some students whispering worriedly, 'Have you seen Parth? Where is he? Sister Stella has been looking for him.' I readied myself to lie and that was, I think, when I completely lost myself. I felt so hollow, as though my mind and heart were encased in stone.

'Madhav, have you seen Parth?' asked Joffin.

I was quiet for a while. 'Umm . . . I . . . I had asked you about him, remember? I don't know where he is. I have not seen him,' I said, fighting back tears.

'He is not in his dormitory,' said a student who came running from the boarding house.

'Nor is he in the library,' said another. News soon spread that Parth had been missing since noon. There was a strange bustle of activity all around the campus. Father George asked the security guards to search the campus premises thoroughly. Some said they had seen Parth walking towards the hilltop and I was afraid somebody had seen me going there too. For a moment, I thought about telling everyone the truth but then I stopped myself. I couldn't face being called a murderer for the rest of my life.

We waited in the boarding house as the faculty and guards went looking for Parth.

The entire school was awake till midnight. The students were told to go to sleep, but everyone refused. I looked up as one of the guards came back and murmured something to Father George.

'They have found his wheelchair near the small hill,' a student said in horror and a whisper ran through the crowd.

I walked away and hid in a corner of the boarding house. I knew that the guards would eventually find Parth and I couldn't bear talking to anyone. I sat in that dark corner of the building for hours, letting his memories wash over me. Perhaps that's when he started taking root in me.

I closed my eyes and screamed silently, over and over again. I was the only one who knew how Parth had died. I felt like an escaped convict. The feeling latched on to my psyche. After a few hours, I saw students running towards the gate. My heart stopped. I stood up and walked that way. Before I could reach the gate, I heard strange howls. The guards and the faculty instructed the students to return to their dorms as an ambulance entered the school premises. The sirens hurt my head.

I saw the guards transfer a body into the van. It was Parth's. The faculty took us all back to the boarding house.

That night, I sat in the bathroom, staring at the white walls. I heard a voice echoing in the bathroom.

'Madhav . . . Madhav . . .' It sounded like Parth. I heard his voice echoing the entire night. I tried to shut my ears, but the voice only grew louder. I rested my head against the wall and closed my eyes.

When I opened them, I saw Parth emerging from the shadows and coming towards me on his wheelchair. His uniform was covered in blood. His head was smashed and bleeding. He stood up and then started laughing at me.

'Why are you here?' I asked him.

'I will always be here. I will never leave you. I will always be with you, inside you,' he whispered as he moved closer and closer until he pushed himself inside my chest and entered my body. I woke up, covered in sweat, below the sink.

There was no one around. That was the first hallucination. I thought it was just a bad dream, not knowing that it would become a part of my life. I left the bathroom. I hadn't realized how long it had been. I walked towards my empty dorm.

'What are you doing here?' a security warden asked me.

'I was just . . .' I stopped short.

'You should be in church,' he reproached.

'Why in church, sir?' I asked.

'This is ridiculous. I thought that crippled boy was your friend,' he said.

'What happened to him?' I was lying to myself now. The warden muttered something and walked away. I was still in my uniform and had not eaten anything since the previous morning. Feeling dizzy, I went to the church. A crowd had gathered in silence and as I stood in line, Father George began speaking.

'It is a sad morning for one and all as we mourn the demise of one of our dear students,' Father George said and I almost fainted. I looked around for Parth. I was in complete denial; I couldn't let him go.

'We are extremely sad for Parth Aggarwal's family and wish to express our condolences to his friends. We deeply regret the incident. I would also like to announce that no student is allowed to go to the hill henceforth. Serious action will be taken if anyone is seen around the area. I would like to ask our senior faculty to say a few lines about the child and then we shall all observe a minute of silence.' He left the podium. It seemed as if a lifetime had passed since I'd seen him fall. But where was his body? Where were his parents? What happened after they found him?

Father Craig, the vice-principal, started speaking. 'Parth was a bright student. Despite his disability, he won scholarships and numerous medals for the school. His contribution will always be remembered. His achievements shall be displayed on the wall of fame in the school.'

Once the ceremony had ended, the students quietly went to the mess for breakfast.

Sister Stella came up to me and asked, 'Where were you, Madhav?' She looked very concerned and upset.

'I am sorry, Sister. I was disturbed . . . so . . .'

She interrupted me, 'I am really sorry. We know this is a big loss. We cannot stop what God has planned for all of us. Accidents cannot be avoided, my child. We are all here for his family and friends. I would suggest you take some time to heal.'

They thought it was an accident! I sighed. 'Where is he now?' I asked.

'His parents came a few hours ago and took his body away for the funeral. The police will investigate the case later. They are under the impression that he committed suicide,' she said, placing her hand on my head, unaware that I was the one behind Parth's death.

I began thinking of myself as a murderer. The guilt grew stronger with each breath I took. As I returned to the dorm, a ward boy told me, Joffin and two other students to report to Father George's office.

It was the second time in two days that I had found myself in that office. I was terrified by what I saw—in the office sat Sister Sophia, Sister Stella, Father George and two police officers. In the cold winter of Nainital, I began sweating, which made it evident that I was scared.

'Come, Madhav,' said Father George, kindly. The four of us sat on the sofa in the corner of the room.

'Officer, this is Madhav Mehra. He was Parth's closest friend at school. You may ask him whatever you want to know.' Father George looked at me and said, 'Son, don't worry, just answer honestly.'

One of the officers said, 'We just want to ask you a few simple questions. When was the last time you saw Parth?'

The officer's question released a flood of memories.

'What's wrong? Why are you sweating?' the officer asked. 'Have some water.'

'I last saw him at dinner the night before,' I said, clearing my throat, trying to sound confident.

'Did he seem disturbed?' asked the other officer.

'No. He'd undergone a knee surgery a few days ago and was in pain, so he went to sleep early,' I replied.

'And the next morning?' the officer asked Joffin.

'I don't know, sir. Parth missed all the morning classes. Even Madhav missed his classes,' he said.

'Why weren't you in class, Madhav?'

I thought for a while before lying. I wasn't sure if the truth would help anyone, but a lie would surely save me from being called a murderer. So I made up a story. 'I was looking for Parth all morning. I even asked Joffin if he had seen him but he hadn't.' Joffin nodded, corroborating the story.

One of our other classmates spoke up, 'But I told you I had seen him walking towards the hill and you went in that direction.' I hadn't expected him to remember our exchange.

'That is true, sir. I went looking for Parth. But I couldn't find him, so I came back,' I said.

'The teachers told us that you and Parth were the only students who didn't attend class that morning,' said the officer.

It was difficult for me to think clearly and weave a credible story due to the turmoil inside me.

'I was looking for him. That's all I have to say, sir,' I murmured.

After an hour's questioning, the officers ruled that Parth's death had been an accident.

The postmortem report did not indicate anything suspicious either because Parth and I did not have a physical confrontation. But I knew I was the culprit. I had taken my friend's life.

Over the next few days, to survive the trauma, I made him a part of me. His dreams became mine, his personality became mine too. I would see Parth all the time. I would feel him sitting next to me, I would hear his voice telling me what to do. I didn't even realize that I had become like him, studying day and night. But in becoming Parth, I had to destroy myself. I forgot about poetry. I stopped writing. I was only focussed on achieving his dreams.

Every time I entered the dorm, I saw Parth on his bed. I saw him playing basketball, smoking up in the sports field, studying in the library. I saw him everywhere. I even took up smoking to be more like him.

I tried filling the chasm inside me with what I had lost. Parth's aggression, violence and hatred were the last things I had witnessed and it was this that drove my new identity.

One day, before the board exams, I was walking past the infirmary when I noticed Parth's wheelchair in a corner. I pulled it out and touched it. I felt his energy flowing through it into me. I took his spectacles out of my bag, where I'd kept them, and put them on. I tried to smile like him too, not knowing what was happening to me.

The spectacles blurred my vision but I kept them on as I sat on the wheelchair. I rolled the wheelchair around the boarding house, laughing, as I felt Parth's identity take over mine. A few students gathered around to watch as I behaved like a lunatic. A whisper ran through the crowd. Within minutes, the guards caught hold of me and brought me back to the infirmary.

There was a lot of talk about my mental health after Parth's demise. There were several people who had witnessed me doing odd things, besides lying, hurting people and even myself at times. The principal decided to terminate my enrolment and send me back to Delhi. My parents were told to take me home after the board exams. But day and night, I toiled, driven by the strange force with which I was becoming familiar. After I topped the board exams, the school reconsidered my expulsion, but my parents decided nevertheless to take me back home.

Shriya didn't even come to see me or speak to me after Parth's death. I heard she moved to London with her family soon after. I never saw or heard of her again.

Since that day, I have always kept Parth's spectacles with me. I wear them whenever I feel the need to be like him, sometimes intentionally, sometimes unknowingly. There is not a single day where I don't curse myself for killing him. Since that day I have been living like this— living two lives, two dreams. While trying to find Parth, I lost myself.

17

6 January 2012

Night had fallen. The hills looked mesmerizing in the moonlight. The wind whipped around Radhika and Madhav.

As she sat next to him on the hilltop, she was amazed at what he had done. He had chosen to adopt Parth's identity. He had chosen to be this way.

Madhav was in tears. Radhika held him tightly.

'This is where he died,' he cried, pointing to the edge of the gorge a few metres away from them.

'You did not kill him, Madhav. It was an accident,' she said gently, but he was unable to wrap his head around her words, having spent so many years believing he was a murderer.

Radhika stood up and walked closer to the edge. She looked up at the moon shining in the velvety sky. Madhav wiped his tears as he saw her moving closer towards the edge.

'Radhika!' he called out. She didn't look back. It was growing darker with each passing second. She walked as though she were blind, not looking down.

'Radhika, stop!' Madhav ran towards her.

She turned back. Their eyes met, as though it were for the last time.

'Radhika, what are you doing? Be careful,' he said. She stood at the edge of the gorge, unresponsive. The wind blew violently as Madhav moved closer to her. She raised a foot and dangled it over the precipice.

He screamed and caught her hand as she went over the edge. She stared at him as he travelled back in time to the moment when he'd been unable to save Parth. His grip on her hand began slipping but she didn't say a word. She just looked into his eyes. Madhav had to save her in order to save himself. He had to pull her back up. He was stronger now but his heart was as weak as it had been eleven years ago. He dug his feet in the mud to get a strong foothold and reached out for Radhika's other hand.

He screamed out her name, his voice echoing through the valley as he pulled her towards him.

Radhika believed in her heart that her plan would work. 'Please save me, Madhav,' she whispered.

Her words rang in his ears. His vision blurred and he saw Parth in front of him instead of Radhika.

'Parth,' he whispered. 'I cannot let you die. I will save you. I will never let you go.' He pulled her up, hugged her tightly and cried, 'I didn't kill you. I never killed you. I saved you. I kept you safe.'

She cradled his head and wiped away his tears. She knew the love she had for him would heal him in a way that therapy never could.

'Each breath we take is an opportunity for a new life, Madhav. Live each day fully and see how beautiful your life becomes.'

They had their arms wrapped around each other as Madhav sobbed. 'I wish I could have told him what he meant to me.'

'He knows, Madhav. He knows how much you miss him,' she said.

'I can feel him,' Madhav whispered fearfully.

'Madhav, let Parth go. He wants to go,' she whispered. 'Let him fly. Do not cage him inside you, Madhav. Let him go. Unless you let him go, forgive yourself and realize that the nightmare is over, you won't be able to move forward or follow your dreams. You need to let go of all that is dragging you down.'

Madhav went to the edge of the gorge. He looked down into the abyss.

'Goodbye, Parth. I will miss you. I know nothing will make you happier than if I lived for myself. I remember you once told me, "Follow your dreams and I will be with you."'

Madhav sighed as he felt the heaviness seep out of him and into the valley below. Radhika hugged him from behind and he turned to kiss her forehead. The bright stars had taken over the sky. As they lay on the grass, Radhika thought, magic happens when you do not give up, even though you want to. The universe will always fall in love with a stubborn heart and will help it find a way.

'You've written poems for everyone, Madhav, but never for me.' Madhav smiled as Radhika pretended to be offended. He had not written for a while but their love would now be his inspiration. He kissed her nose and the words came to him.

> The story has just begun
> Love knows no end,
> All it knows are beginnings.
> This is where our love begins,
> From now till eternity.

Love had finally found its way, like it always did. Madhav sat on his knees, looking straight into her eyes, presenting his poem as a ring to Radhika. 'I don't know what is right and wrong. What I do know is that I love you and it is the most honest, pure thing I have ever felt in my life. Will you marry me, Radhika?'

Epilogue

10 July 2016
Haldwani

The train halted at Haldwani railway station. We were already at the Kumaon foothills. I was quiet, my eyes moist. The woman had finished her tale. We had not realized that it had been six hours. Gitanjali was sitting in the same position, with a slight smile on her face. Her green eyes gleamed as tears caressed her cheeks. I sighed and looked at the woman who was smiling wistfully.

'What happened next? Did she say yes? Are they married now?' Gitanjali asked. There was no end to our curiosity after hearing this incredible tale of love, loss and friendship.

'Is it a true story?' The writer in me was dying to know.

'Friends, we have reached our station,' the woman said and picked up her bag.

'But we want to know what happened next. I mean, where are they now? Are they together?' Gitanjali asked.

'You're going to Nainital, right?' she asked, looking at us.

'Yes, we are!' I said.

'If you want to know what happened next, you will have to come with me.'

'Where?'

'You will see. Don't worry, I am not going to kidnap you,' she said with a smirk. We packed our stuff and got off the train.

We followed the woman and got into a taxi. Nainital was an hour's drive away. We both were curious and anxious. The car moved up the foothills as Haldwani sparkled like a Christmas tree below us.

As we drove up to a beautiful cottage nestled at the top of a small hill, the woman asked the driver to stop the car. We could see the serene Naini Lake below us.

'Is this your home?' Gitanjali asked.

'Yes,' said the woman, getting out to ring the doorbell. It wasn't a usual door bell. It was a Swiss cowbell, just like the one at Radhika's home in the story. There was something fishy going on. On a wooden plaque next to the door was an inscription: Love will find a way.

'Open the door, honey!' she said, sweetly.

A man opened the door. He was tall and handsome, with a thick beard. He smiled as the woman hugged him. 'How was your journey, baby?' he asked and looked at us questioningly.

'We have guests, Madhav,' the woman said and our jaws dropped.

Gitanjali stared at them as if someone had taken the wind out of her sails.

The woman turned to us and said, 'My name is Radhika. Why don't you come in?'

Stunned, Gitanjali and I stood at the door like mannequins.

'We will not eat you! Come inside,' Madhav said.

We entered their beautiful and warm home. We saw a painting in the living room, the one Radhika had described—two boys in school uniforms, one in a wheelchair and the other with his arm around him.

We also saw their photograph. My brain froze for a couple of seconds and Gitanjali was speechless. The room was full of beautiful paintings. There was a huge wedding photograph right above the fireplace. We were overjoyed to see it. They had finally been united in love.

'I was surprised when you guys didn't even ask my name,' Radhika said.

Madhav was making coffee, oblivious to the fact that we had just heard his life story.

'Has my wife been regaling you with her tales?' Madhav asked as he placed a bowl of dry fruit on the table. 'She is a visiting professor at Delhi University and often travels to Delhi for work,' he said.

'We know! We know! What about psychotherapy?' Gitanjali asked.

'I left it as I failed to choose between love and ethics,' Radhika said and hugged Madhav. 'And he is a poet. He is also passionate about organic farming nowadays.' I felt joyful seeing them together.

'Where is your mother?' Gitanjali asked Madhav.

'How do you know her?'

'Radhika shared a bit of your life story,' she said.

'She lives in Delhi with my father,' Madhav said. 'We moved to Nainital a year after our wedding.'

'And Madhav's sister lives in the States. My parents now live in my old office in Delhi. They returned from London when we got married.' Radhika answered all our nosy questions. We wanted to talk to them for hours.

'So are you guys married?' Madhav asked us.

'We are planning to get married but he has not proposed to me yet,' Gitanjali said and they laughed.

Radhika came up to me and whispered in my ear, 'Just tell her what Madhav said to me.'

'I will.' I said and winked at her.

Before Gitanjali and I could continue on our journey, there was another surprise in store for us.

We heard footsteps behind us. As we turned around, we saw a small boy running down the stairs. He wore a cute woollen cap and a yellow jacket with white pyjamas. He hugged Radhika and she kissed his cheeks. He then went to Madhav.

'Daddy, Daddy, look! I wrote a poem for Mumma and you,' the little boy said, his voice incredibly sweet.

'That's beautiful, Parth.'

Acknowledgements

I believe this is the most special page of this book as it has gratitude for all those who have actually made it happen. First and foremost, I would like to thank God. In the process of putting this book together I realized how much this gift of writing means to me.

To my guru, who has given me the power to believe in my passion and pursue my dreams. I could never have done this without the faith I have in you. To my parents, I can barely find the words to express my gratitude for all the wisdom, love and support you've given me. If I am blessed to live long enough, I hope I can be as good as you are. To my sisters, Vidhi and Purti, for being there. Your love keeps me going. I would never have come so far without you both by my side.

As always, I thank my beautiful partner in crime, Gitanjali, for not only being my storyteller but also for giving me so much energy and love. I am so thankful to have you in my life and for pushing me when I am ready to give up. Without you, this story would not have seen the light of day. My words are the proof of the beauty I see when I look into your eyes.

I would also like to thank Mohnish, Sahil and all my friends for always being there, and kindly putting up with me. A big thanks to Devanshi, Kunal and Abbas for listening to the story, Linda, Arjun and Nimish for the magical pictures and Sohail, Pari, Komal, Fiza and all our wonderful Kat-Katha children for the prayers.

I would like to express my gratitude to the entire team at Penguin Random House, to all those who read and assisted in the editing, proofreading and design of the book. Very special gratitude goes out to my editor, Gurveen Chadha, for challenging me to do better and for helping me shape this book.

Most important of all, thanks to my readers for taking out time to write to me. Your emails, reviews, messages and comments encourage me to do better. I think I must have the most loveliest and generous readers in the world. I also seek forgiveness from all those who have been with me for all these years and whose names I have failed to mention.

In the end, I request each one of you to listen to the unheard stories of people around them as it might heal their hearts and help them overcome a difficult phase in life. We are all one big family after all! So keep sharing, smiling and spreading love for it will surely find a way.